Farewell Party

Also by June Drummond

FAREWELL PARTY

June Drummond

A RED BADGE NOVEL OF SUSPENSE

Dodd, Mead & Company · New York

First published in the United States 1973

ISBN: 0-396-06624-0
Library of Congress Catalog Card Number: 72-7921
Printed in the United States of America

I

It was the night of Errol Hoburn's twenty-first birthday that I began to wonder whether my aunt Kate Falconer was really dead. If you can still dictate people's lives twenty years after your official obituary, then you may be dead but you certainly aren't buried.

Perhaps my feeling about Kate had been building up for a long time. When I came back from Europe last year I opened her shack down on Kolumbe estuary, and started to operate her kilns again. Working where she'd worked sort of brought her alive for me. All my life I'd been encouraged to forget about her. Now suddenly I was being forced to remember her and I didn't much like it.

I liked it even less after the article appeared in the *Chronicle*, the bit about the Michael Crescent property.

I'm not being very clear.

Let me go back and explain. I live at Kolumbe farm, about forty miles from Durban. My family once owned a town house in Michael Crescent, which is part of the suburb known as Peak Hill.

At the beginning of May, on Friday 8th to be exact, an article appeared on the town-planning page of the *Chronicle*, saying that the proposed scheme for the development of Peak Hill was under way. The plans included three blocks of flats, a community hall, offices, and a new church to replace St. Michael and All Angels. The article went on to say that no shopping centre would be built because the one in existence "on the old Falconer property in Michael Crescent" was considered big enough to serve the district.

Then came the paragraphs with the sting: "This shopping centre has been a source of bitter dispute among the residents of Peak Hill for nearly a quarter of a century. The Falconer land became available through a set of tragic circumstances. It was the untimely death of Deirdre Bryant, one of the lovely Falconer twins, that made her husband Ralph Bryant owner of the house. The subsequent disappearance and presumed death of the second sister, Kate Falconer, and the attendant scandal, drove Mr Bryant to quit Michael Crescent and offer the entire five-acre site to a development company.

"Despite the protests of the inhabitants of the Crescent, and lengthy litigation between them and the company promoters, the shopping centre was eventually built. It seems that the latest plans for Peak Hill will complete the erosion of the suburb, which until now has retained its character as a picturesque corner of old Durban. It could be said that this is one of the saddest consequences to flow from the still-unsolved riddle of the disappearance of Kate Falconer, who vanished without trace on October 30th 1946. It is to be hoped that the new excavations do not exhume the ancient feuds."

There was nothing new to me in all this. Polly told me the whole story when I was quite young. Polly is my father's sister and she brought me up and was always the one I thought of as my mother. My own mother, the Deirdre of the newspaper article, died of encephalitis when I was seven months old. That was in the Michaelmas of 1945. Kate was away in England, exhibiting some of her work. She came back as fast as she could, but with the war just over, travel was difficult even for urgent reasons, and by the time she reached home my mother was dead. Polly always said her death was the reason Kate was so unstable in the last year of her life.

And then in October 1946, Kate herself vanished. Her sailing dinghy was found wedged in the reeds on Kolumbe estuary, and the inquest presumed that she'd taken the boat out and somehow overturned it and been drowned. The river was in flood and the tide at the spring, so that kind of accident could have happened very easily.

Ralph Bryant, my father, couldn't stand the Michael Crescent house after that. He sold out his business interests, moved to Kolumbe farm, fetched Polly from the Highveld to look after me, and settled into the rural scene. He liked running the farm and became quite good at it. When I was eight he was killed in a level-crossing smash. Again, that can happen all too easily on the farmlands. I mean, I've never felt my family was ill-starred or anything like that. But I admit the newspapers have played up the Greek tragedy bit. That's why it upset me, seeing the story in the *Chronicle*. I thought, oh hell they're at it again.

My father didn't belong in heavy drama. He was tall, fair, and usually wore a bewildered smile. I loved him, but quite early on I knew I couldn't rely on him for practical things. He was the sort of man who's so close to being childish that he knows exactly what children enjoy. He showed me how to make farmyard animals from the river clays, red for the cattle and hens, white for the pigs and ducks. I have the set still, my first models.

So I grew up on the farm. We grow sugar, Kolumbe is all sugar country, but the estuary can't be cultivated. The sour lands run in a mile-wide belt on each side of the river, and down by the mouth the ground rises sharply in a bluff covered with bush. All that is useless for farming, but perfect for a bird sanctuary, and that's why my grandfather Sidney Falconer bought it.

The story goes he paid for it with a year's gambling gains; but Polly says that's bunkum, that he was a shrewdie who never gambled unless the odds were running his way. He certainly made a lot of money in his lifetime. He spread it about, too. For instance, he made Kolumbe Bird Sanctuary a company, kept two-thirds of the shares but made the rest available to the people of the village. He said they ought to have a stake in it.

Kolumbe is one of the most beautiful places I've seen, and I've seen quite a big piece of the world in the five years I've travelled and studied pottery. About a year ago, I got tired of moving and decided it was time to come home. I knew I could work at Kolumbe. There's plenty of clay of all colours and grades, and Kate's kilns are sound. I wanted very much to make a proper study of her working notes, learn her techniques of glazing and firing. I'll never be as good as she was, but there's no reason why I can't have the same technical knowledge.

7

Then, I must be honest, I needed to sort things out. For two years I'd been entangled ... that's the right word ... with a journalist and the last six months we fought each other to a standstill. It was over but I was still kind of waiting for the dust to settle so I could see where I was going.

That's why I never took Errol Hoburn seriously. He just seemed a lonely kid who'd been a neighbour ever since I could remember. I went riding with him, or to the beach. He was four years younger than me and was supposed to be learning how to run the Hoburn farm. He was very unhappy and often said he wanted to go to the Rand and become a mining engineer. When he talked about turning twenty-one and being able to do as he pleased, I certainly didn't think I figured in his plans.

The evening of his birthday party began happily. I went down to the shack about six o'clock to collect the present I'd made him. It was a flamingo, conventional but I thought pretty good. I'd used red clay and left the glaze thin in parts so that at certain angles the colour shone through. When I took it off the shelf I liked it so much I almost decided to keep it. Then I remembered how miserable Errol was, and the useless way he spent his days, and I wrapped the flamingo up and put it with my evening bag. It was still too early to leave, so I went out on to the big verandah that overhangs the river.

The shack is most beautifully placed. My grandfather built it of hardwoods on a spur of land that juts out into the estuary. The bush runs right up to the back door, but the front we keep cleared so that you can look up and down the river and across the sandbar at the mouth to the sea beyond. That was a great sunset. Not a lot of colour but a wash of peach-green that ran across the sky as smooth as silence. All the marshland to the west was studded with pampas grass that burned like a procession of torches, and I could see the cane fields west again, undulating in long silky waves as the offshore breezes began to blow.

I sat looking over the estuary. After a while I fetched the binoculars and studied the tufty scrub on Kolumbe island in midstream, and the cliffs far away on the opposite bank. They

8

have a hunched, quiet shape. Perhaps that's why the Zulus say the estuary is *tagati*, bewitched, and won't come near it.

Just before seven o'clock I saw the Pel's fishing-owl that moved into our territory last month. Big as an eagle-owl and with a terrific wing-span, he wheeled across the river-mouth and flew straight over the shack. I could see the prickly pads on his feet for holding fish.

I didn't want to leave, but it was time to make the Hoburn revels. I drove back along our side of the river to where it narrows, and crossed over the bridge to the Hoburns' farm. The house was blazing with lights and there was a huge marquee on the lawn with a bar and a dance-floor, but nobody had arrived yet.

I drove round to the back and parked the Volvo and went in through the kitchen door. Several of the African farm-workers were there, including big Nigewe the tractor-foreman in a long white coat and white gloves. I asked him if he was the new Minister and he laughed and said no, he was the Praise-maker. He rolled out my name, Miss Leonora Bryant, and added a string of high-sounding Zulu titles. I stayed talking a bit and then went through into the house. I wanted to say hello to Errol and give him his present, so I went along the corridor and knocked on the door of his room.

There's a long mirror in the angle of the hall and I could see myself as I walked up to it. Looking in a glass isn't much cop when you're tall and skimpy and have red hair and the Falconer nose, but that night I felt I looked quite good. I had on a white dress I brought back from Paris and for once my hair was staying where I put it.

The door opened and I started forward with the big birthday hug and kiss, but to my surprise Errol almost slammed the door on me. He stood there with bulging eyes and said, "Lennie! Didn't you get my message?"

"No, I've been down at the shack. What was it?"

"Not to come."

For a moment I could only think that something dreadful had happened, a shooting-accident or somebody dead so they couldn't hold the party. Then I remembered the Zulus in the

9

kitchen and knew it wasn't death. I said, "What's happened, whatever's the matter?"

Errol stretched his arm across the doorway in a very dramatic way. "I don't want you here tonight. I can't explain now, I'll tell you tomorrow."

Well, then it was my turn to stare. I just couldn't get the thread at all. I started to speak and he threw up his arms and said with real desperation, "For God's sake Lennie, go away. I can't bear any more." And he rushed back into his room and shut the door.

There didn't seem to be much to do but leave. I started back along the hall. I was at the kitchen door when I changed my mind and marched round to the far side of the house where Mr and Mrs Hoburn have their rooms. I thought at least I'd say goodnight to them. But as soon as Carla Hoburn opened her door and I saw the surprise and displeasure on her face I realised I was taking part in a feud.

Carla is a handsome woman, fair and neat like Errol, but at that moment she looked dishevelled. She was dressed for the ball but hadn't put on her make-up. Her lips had a mauve colour as if she were cold.

I said, "Carla, could I speak to you?"

She barred my way just as Errol had done. "Much better not, Leonora."

I began to feel angry. "Why is everything so odd? Have I done something?"

"There is nothing we need discuss." That was a lie. She was just dying to yell at me, I could see.

"Why did Errol ask me to go home?"

"We think it's best. We don't want to spoil the evening for our guests."

"I thought I was one of them."

She gave me a glance that was almost shifty. It was strange. She wasn't the woman I'd known all my life. She watched me in that queer way and then she stepped back and jerked the door wide. "All right. Come in. We'll settle this once and for all."

Inside her bedroom she moved back and forth as if she

couldn't stop. She kept her back to me and said, "It's a pity that you and Errol have been so sly about this, Leonora. A little more honesty and we'd all have been spared a great deal of unhappiness."

"I don't understand. I gather you've quarrelled with Errol?"

"Oh, now don't take the high line with me, young lady." She spun round and wagged a finger. "None of your sophisticated double-talk here! Errol told me the whole story. You must have led him on, all right. He's years younger than you, a child in some ways."

"I agree."

But Carla wasn't concerned with what I felt. She kept pacing, pacing, and with every step she seemed to get wilder and wilder.

"We've always been so close, Errol and I. He's never lied to me, always told me everything. Time and again I've questioned him about you and every time he's told me, 'There's nothing to it, we're friends, that's all.' And you've come to our home as mealy-mouthed as a parson's daughter, abused our trust, encouraged Errol to deceive us. You've made a fool of him, all right. You know he has no money, he's delicate, he can't even hope to run the farm for years yet, how can he talk of marriage?"

Light began to dawn. "There's no need to worry," I told her, "Errol is just looking for the right sort of work. He's not thinking of marriage at all."

"Lies! Lies! He admitted he'd already asked you."

"Then I'm afraid I didn't recognise his meaning or I'd certainly have given him a plain answer."

"I've no doubt of that. With your record I should think you'd jump at a decent boy like Errol. Well, let me tell you that rather than have him marry a member of your family, I'd sell this farm and move to the farthest point of the globe."

I began to turn away from her, but she sidled round and blocked my path. "You've tricked him, but you haven't tricked me. I'll open his eyes, don't worry. I'll tell him every single thing I can about your holy Falconer tribe. A mother who was crazy, walked barefoot in the village, talked to birds! A father who drank himself sodden. An aunt everyone knew was the town bitch. If all that's going to be in the papers again then I'm not having Errol mixed up in it. You're not the sort of girl my boy's going to marry, you can get that into your head once and for all. Now it's best if you go away and stay away. I don't want to see you here again."

She was half-crazy. She jerked her hand and it struck the parcel I was holding. I felt the flamingo's neck snap under the wrappings, and suddenly I was as furious as she was.

"Carla, I don't give a damn whether I come here or not. But if I were you I'd stop deciding Errol's life for him. He's miserable as hell and one of these days he's going to get sick of you and walk out."

"Get away from me. Get out." She was yelling and shaking and there was a blue look all round her mouth.

I walked out of the house as calmly as I could but when I climbed into the Volvo my legs trembled so much I could hardly get her moving.

When I reached home, Polly came out on the stoep to meet me. She took one look at me and came running down the steps.

"Darling, what's wrong?"

"Nothing. It's quite all right."

"That Carla. She said something, didn't she? What did she say to you?"

"Threw me out of the house."

Polly started to mutter under her breath. We went into the kitchen and she slammed the coffee pot on to the stove and watched it bubble up, and poured two big cups laced with brandy and cream. As I started to drink she said, "You don't feel anything for Errol, do you?"

"I'd like to wring his bloody little neck. He must have let Carla think I meant to marry him."

"I expect he just wanted to hurt her."

"That's nice."

"Those two are mean, Lennie. Errol's a mess. He's never going to escape from her. And she's pure poison. I should have warned you as soon as you came home, but you seemed to like Errol, and I didn't want to make trouble."

I finished my coffee and then told Polly the whole tale. At the end I said, "It was the way she attacked my family. As if we spent our time in the yellow press. I just so nearly hit that female."

Polly said nothing for a while and then she hitched her chair forward. "You get this clear, love. Your father did not drink himself sodden. He drank fairly heavily just after Deirdre died, but not after he came out here. The accident that killed him happened at nine in the morning and the police report exonerated him of all blame.

"As for your mother, she did go barefoot sometimes and she did talk to birds. That's nothing. You know perfectly well you all do that."

"What about Aunt Kate, the Bitch of Durban?"

Polly shook her head. "You had to know Kate very well to understand her, to appreciate her. She did some crazy things."

"Was she crazy?"

"No. More sane than most of us, perhaps. She had a different set of values. No hypocrisy. She made terrible mistakes about people, but not about herself. She was never taken in by the Kate in the mirror. If she'd been less honest, she might have lived longer."

"Why do you say that?"

"You can't run head-on into life as she did, and survive. She took too many risks. But at least now they might let her rest."

She got up and carried the cups over to the sink and dumped them in with a bang.

"You're thinking about this piece in the *Chronicle*?" I said.

"I suppose half Natal is. Someone dreamed it up. Why? Why not let her sleep? But no, they have to probe and dig and pry. What good does it do? What good did it ever do? I warned them at the time, Ralph and the others, let it lie. What can you get from all those questions, doubts, the Corbitts saying she'd gone off with a man, Ralph hating them for it, all the trouble! I knew they'd never find out what happened to her. I know Kolumbe River. You know what it's like at flood tide."

"You believe Kate was drowned?"

"Yes, I do."

"Do you think she killed herself?"

13

"Never! I told you, she never compromised. She never killed herself, and she never walked out on anyone, believe that. The reason she didn't come home to you and Ralph was that she was dead. It's wicked to say anything else. I told them over and over again. I wouldn't talk to those reporters in the end. Blowing on the rumours until they were raging fires. Your father suffered enough. It was seven years before they could presume her death. Imagine what those years were like for Ralph."

Polly gave me a sudden glance and her face smoothed out. She said in quite a different voice, "Tomorrow morning I'm driving over to give Carla Hoburn a piece of my mind."

"No you aren't. You're going to Port Elizabeth for the bowls tournament, as you planned."

"I can't leave you alone now."

"Why not? Forget Carla, forget Kate. I'm going to."

That was a lie.

I felt too restless to go to bed, so I changed into jeans and a leather jacket and went into the garden. I strolled about a bit, thinking of what the Hoburns had said, and Polly too. Their words went round and round in my head and I began to see that the argument had been going on all my life, among the people I knew. There was one set of voices spreading tales about my relations, and another set trying to hush them up. The trouble was that both sets had the same effect. They stamped my family out of mind as real human beings, and left something distorted.

So from feeling angry, I began to feel cheated. I walked about the garden a bit more and then I went down to the barn to say goodnight to Freya. Freya is a Peregrine Falcon. When she was barely fledged some poacher on the sour lands shot her full of pellets and James Bourne our head warden gave her to me to look after. Since then she's counted the acres round our house as her territory. I'm training her to work from the wrist. She's not a nocturnal hunter, of course, so I didn't expect to find her very lively, but I went to the barn door and whistled. When I heard movement inside I pulled my leather sleeve well down, opened the door, and whistled again. She came across with a rustle of wings and landed on my forearm.

I carried her outside and she blinked in the moonlight, turning her splendid golden stare over the garden and the sugar-fields. I talked to her a bit and she twisted her head and looked at me.

Carla Hoburn had said my mother was crazy because she talked to birds. There's nothing crazy in that. All my family does. We work with birds because that's something we can do, the way other people can bake samoosas, or divine water, or tread the high wire. Our name, Falconer, shows how old the trade is with us. That's why my grandfather was ready to tie up capital in the bird sanctuary. A wilderness is one of the most expensive things to maintain. To protect birds you have to protect the whole natural cycle, including flora and fauna, and you need hard cash to fight off the people who want to plant money crops or run a road through or start a caravan park.

Standing by the barn I thought that was one thing I knew about my mother. She was sane enough to know the difference between an ostrich and an osprey.

Then I started thinking about Kate, and I saw I knew her too, because of her work. It was there, I'd seen it, not only in my own home and at the shack, but in some of the best modern collections in Europe and America. Her work has integrity and imagination, and tremendous technical skill. It's not the work of a nothing. I knew why I'd been feeling guilty all these months. I'd allowed myself to pretend Kate was better dead, and that's the worst thing you can say about anyone, especially about an artist with a load of work to do.

"Well Freya," I said, "what's next?"

She half-bated, flexing her talons on my wrist and arching her wings. A Peregrine will quarrel with an eagle on occasion. I knew what Freya would make of Carla Hoburn and the other little shrikes.

"Go a-hunting, shall I?"

A name was bothering me, one Polly muttered when she

was dumping the cups in the sink. Garbutt? Corbitt? I hadn't heard her mention it before.

Far away across the river I could see the lights of Errol's birthday party. They didn't mean a thing. I took Freya back to the barn and left her there. I'd made up my mind that once Polly was on the train for Port Elizabeth, I'd try and find out who put the article about Michael Crescent into the *Chronicle*.

ᔊ ᔊ ᔊ

II

As soon as I'd waved Polly off at Durban station, I drove up to the flat and left my things. We keep the flat as a town base and although it's only three rooms it's in an old block right on top of the Ridge and there's plenty of space.

The person I wanted to see first was Evan Cruikshank. He's an old friend of ours, an icthyologist. He says he prefers fish to humans but he knows a lot about both species. Polly says he'd have been murdered long ago if his memoirs weren't locked up at the Bank, ready to be published on his death. He's also a director of the *Chronicle*.

He was difficult to find. I caught up with him about three that afternoon, standing on the south beach in a high wind, quarrelling with two civil servants about water pollution. When he'd dealt with them he turned to me and said snappishly, "Hully, Lennie, what do you want? Won't find any birds here, you know. All dead of oil and filth." At that moment a particularly plump tern swerved overhead. Evan gave it a poisonous look and stumped up

16

the beach to the promenade. I followed and asked if I could talk to him.

"You can come with me to the aquarium," he said, "I'll give you a lift."

"I'm not letting you drive me anywhere."

"Lily-livered like the rest."

"Evan, last year you were fined for driving that German tenor up the steps of the City Hall."

"Down. It was down. I've never heard anyone scream so well, excellent tone throughout the range. Well, we can have tea across the road. It'll taste of effluent, everything does around here, but that's your lookout."

We went over to the café and found a table. As soon as the tea arrived Evan fixed his squinty little eyes on me and said, "So Lennie, what's your case?"

"There was a piece in Friday's *Chronicle* about Michael Crescent. I want to know who wrote it."

Evan shovelled sugar into his cup. "Damn silly article. I shall tell 'em so. I can't stand that property page, who wants to read about real estate?"

"Estate agents, I suppose."

"My darling Leonora, it's not worth worrying about. Forget the whole thing." He looked so apprehensive I knew he might easily clam up altogether.

"I'm not worried, I'm interested. After all, I was born in the Crescent. I've often wondered what it was like in the old days."

Evan didn't answer at once. He sat hunching his shoulders and scowling at the rain that now rattled the windows. At last he said in a flat voice, "Michael Crescent was a cul-de-sac, a dead end, a retreat for the last colonials. Not my sort of world."

"Whose then?"

"Ah, comfortable men in the professions, traders who'd built up fat bank balances. It was Grade A cream. Every house stood on at least an acre of ground. Trees, with great slabs of creeper in flower. Shrubs imported from Jamaica, India, Brazil. One place had huge bamboo thickets at the gate, the mosquitoes were crazy about it.

"It was always very still along the Crescent. Funny trick of the air currents, I suppose. You couldn't see a single building from the roadway. They had privacy. Lost it, too, through their own greed. They should have allowed reasonable sub-division. Instead, they shut the world out. Now those big acreages are jam for the development companies. Soon there'll be multiple blocks all over Peak Hill and it'll only be a matter of time before Michael Crescent goes. It's nothing now but a pebble in a giant's shoe. In five years there'll be ticky-tacky patios and Blue Baby Pools wherever you look. I'm glad your mother never saw her home pulled down."

"What was it like?"

"A steep white place with views of the sea. Your grandfather was a big man and he liked big rooms. He could furnish as he pleased, his wife having died young, and it was all heavy woods and strong colours, crimson and yellow and blue. He was a colourful man himself with florid cheeks. Fine teeth and an easy laugh. The house was always crowded. His friends were farmers, officials, bird people, gamblers and the Turf. He liked music. It was nothing unusual to find a visiting celebrity beating hell out of the grand piano and a poker-player snoring underneath it. The place reeked of tobacco and whisky and verbena soap.

"Every summer the old boy would take the girls off to Kolumbe for a holiday. When they came back, there'd be a party. When I think of the Falconers I think of parties, the Christmas tree and the ball for racing people on July Handicap night, and the bonfire at Hallowe'en. Hallowe'en was always something special. There'd be favours for every guest, fireworks, pumpkins with candles inside. I used to look forward to it as a child and even when I grew up. But the last years, I was out of touch. Drifted away." Evan's eyes looked a long way past me.

"The girls," I said, "what were they like?"

He half-smiled. "Terrifying."

"Beautiful?"

"No, but fascinating. Unexpected. You never knew what they'd do next. They weren't identical twins, but they seemed to share the same spirit. Fire by day and fire by night. Your mother, Deirdre was rather delicate, almost transparent, she'd

18

scorch your heart almost before you knew she was there. Kate was more like her father, with colour in her cheeks and dark red hair. A hearth of coals or a forest blaze, depending how she liked you."

"And she was drowned. 'Water, water, quench fire'."

Evan's head jerked. "Don't talk like that, Lennie."

"Isn't it time someone talked? I'm twenty-five and I've never troubled to find out how Kate died. That's strange if you like. Stranger still that no friend has ever spoken to me of her, all these years. I wonder why?"

"To save you distress."

"Or perhaps they think I'm like her? One of the crazy Falconers who must be handled carefully?" As Evan stared at me wordlessly, I leaned towards him. "Tell me, now. Why did the Corbitts spread the story that Kate ran away with a man?"

III

"WHO TOLD YOU that?" Evan's voice was quite sharp with annoyance.

"Polly. It slipped out, and why not? What's so secret about these people?"

"The Corbitts were part of a feud that lasted years. No one in their right mind would want it to start up again."

"Some facts might emerge."

"Facts? There were no bloody facts!"

A thick green gloom was spreading through the café and a

waiter went round snapping on lights. It didn't seem to make the place any cosier.

"Tell me about Michael Crescent," I said. "All the people who lived there."

"I don't remember. For God's sake, it's twenty years."

"If you won't tell me, Evan, I'll go elsewhere. I'll check the micro-files at the library. I'll go to the police. I'll put an advertisement in every paper in the country."

He sat there shaking his head at me and I watched him and after a while his expression changed. He said quietly, "Very well, Lennie, but I don't know what good it'll do you. Most of the old residents have moved in the last year or so. Still, for what it's worth . . . on the right hand corner as you turned in from Peak Road, were the Malcolms. The Sindig house was next, then Appleyard the ships' chandler. Then a name I don't recall . . . Dawson, Harrison, something like that.

"On the left hand corner was St. Michael and All Angels, with the vicarage behind. Mr Lyte was vicar in those days. He had five children we used to call the Lesser Lytes. Of course I didn't live in the Crescent, but I met them all through the church. Your grandfather was a regular church-goer, and so were my parents. When they died I was on my own, and Sidney Falconer put me through school, and left a sum in his will to send me to university. He was the sort of man who knew every need of his community. He was a good man. If he'd lived, there'd have been none of the trouble that came to us.

"Next to the vicarage there was the Mumfords' double-storey which was very uncomfortable, and their stables, very comfortable. Then the Lenfernas who came from Mauritius about the turn of the century; Dr and Mrs Trolley; and the Corbitts.

"The Falconers had a huge piece of ground at the end of the cul-de-sac, four or five acres curving right round the shoulder of Peak Hill to rejoin Peak Road. That double frontage was what made it so valuable.

"Old Sidney and Josh Corbitt were gambling cronies. Sidney was wealthy but Josh never had the nous to stop playing when his luck was out. He was often in low water. If the brandy hadn't carried him off at a moment when he was relatively flush, the Corbitts might have had to sell up. As it was, they managed to hang on until Nell Corbitt married Derek Sharvey. He set them on their feet again. Sharvey was a clever young man.

"The Falconer and Corbitt children grew up together. They were always through the fence and into each other's houses. There was Deirdre and Kate Falconer, Gretha and Nell Corbitt, and the one boy, Nick. I often thought that was the start of Nick's problem, too many women.

"Those five children were the core of the neighbourhood gang, and as we grew up they remained the centre of our little world. It wasn't just wealth. It was the combination of their individual personalities. They were self-sufficient, remote, but a constellation in our patch of sky. I think their unity was uneasy, though. Formed more by proximity than kinship. Deirdre and Kate were independent and adventurous, always on the hunt for new experience and knowledge. They had a great many friends, mostly men. Nick and Nell Corbitt were quite different, perhaps because their childhood was so very uncertain.

"I don't say they weren't attractive. Nell was the most elegant woman I ever met, tall and slim and absolutely sure in every movement she made. Nick had the same physical grace. He was a fine athlete, before the war and arthritis crippled him. But the Corbitts were loners. Didn't like close relationships. They were extremely conventional, suspicious of innovation whether it was in art or science or the society they led. Just didn't like change. Their talents were purely social and they needed a fixed backdrop.

"Their house was very beautiful, in the French colonial style, and it was always perfectly maintained, even at times when rumour said the Corbitts were down and out. I believe they put that house above everything. It was a symbol to them. If it went, they were finished. And somehow the rest of us came to feel that the whole of Michael Crescent would go with them. It would be the end of the world.

"The other thing that linked the Corbitts to the Falconers, was business. Your father and Derek Sharvey, who married Nell Corbitt, were partners in an agency for building materials. Just before the war they did a deal with Sidney Falconer, and met his daughters. Within weeks they'd both made a bid for Deirdre. Ralph got her. It didn't take Derek long to recover, he married Nell a short while afterwards and it was thought a good match. He wanted her status, she wanted his money, and they seemed to get along very well.

"The strange thing was that neither Ralph nor Derek succeeded in moving his bride from the Crescent. Partly it was because of the war. Ralph was in the Navy, Derek and Nick Corbitt in the army, it seemed best for the womenfolk to stay where they were. Then in 1942 old Sidney died of cancer of the throat. He left a bad will. The town house went to Deirdre, but most of the money to Kate. Kolumbe farm they shared. It meant that Deirdre owned a property she couldn't afford to keep up, except by drawing money from the farm. They had equal shares in the sanctuary, but that was hardly a paying proposition.

"When Ralph came home, late in 1944, there was talk of selling the house, but nothing came of it. Nell Sharvey begged them not to sell. She had lots of troubles then, and counted on the Bryants for help and advice. So Ralph and Deirdre stayed. Kate made the place her base whenever she was in town, and also helped to maintain it. She wasn't often there, however. She was working on the collection of work she meant to take to Europe. Apart from that, she travelled all over Southern Africa, to get the pigments and minerals she needed. She'd go off without warning and be away for weeks at a time. Sometimes she went alone, sometimes she took a companion. She was a law unto herself.

"The Corbitts hung on in Michael Crescent, by the skin of their teeth. Nell had closed up most of the rooms in 1940. She kept one servant to care for the garden and did all the housework herself. Several people tried to buy her out, but she always refused. She said it would be impossible for Nick and Gretha to live anywhere else. Perhaps she believed that. Perhaps it was true. Certainly, when Nick came back we were glad the house was there waiting. He'd been three years in prison-camps, had a bad time because he'd organised several large-scale breaks. When he was shipped home he weighed just over a hundred and thirty pounds. It was a year before he was anything like normal, and the arthritis in his hands was so bad he couldn't dress himself. "Nell found a man to look after him, a sergeant from Nick's battalion. God knows how they paid the doctors' bills. Probably didn't. The one thing that got them through that time was being in Michael Crescent, and among friends.

"Derek Sharvey was the last to arrive back. He took to civilian life in one long, flat, racing dive. There was a building boom and he made money so fast there was no question of the Corbitts having to sell up.

"So there they all were, Corbitts and Falconers, safe and sound in Michael Crescent. It was a false security. When you were born I told Ralph, told him to get Deirdre and you out, but he never did. He tried, but he couldn't hope to stand against the rest of them."

Evan fell silent, moving one finger slowly back and forth along the edge of the table. "The parties started again, crowds of people every night, the whole damn circus. There were plenty of us just home from the war, ready to live it up. But with old Sidney gone, something vital was missing. Humour, balance, I don't know. I didn't like the new friends Sharvey brought in. Seemed a lot of wide boys to me. I warned Ralph to watch them, but warnings never do much good. He was angry with me, we had the helluva quarrel and after that I didn't go to the Crescent very often. Particularly once Kate had gone overseas.

"That was late in 1945. Her first exhibition was a terrific success. There was talk of her staying over, but at Michaelmas your mother fell ill. Ralph sent for Kate. By the time she reached home, Deirdre was dead.

"Kate moved into the old house to look after Ralph and you. Ralph was all to pieces. So was Kate, but it affected her differently. Ralph was quiet, Kate had a sort of wildness, a glitter that wasn't at all healthy. She lived at a tremendous pace, work and play. Her moods were almost hysterical, up in the clouds or down in the depths. She couldn't sleep, and she had to have company all the time. Sometimes she'd go off to the shack and slave for days, until she was so tired she couldn't stand, and then she'd swallow sleeping-pills and sleep for twenty-four hours solid.

"But by the winter of 1946, she seemed to be getting over it. I saw her often, although I still wasn't on the old terms with Ralph. She was calmer, spent a lot of time with you, began to make plans for the future. In September she went to the mountains for two weeks and came back bursting with health, happier than I'd ever seen her. Everything was set fair.

"Then in October, she disappeared. Walked out of the house one evening and never came back.

"For a couple of days, no one worried. We were used to her erratic habits. Ralph thought she'd gone to Kolumbe for the week-end. Then he 'phoned the farm and was told she'd never arrived there. He went to the police and the search began. They found her boat in the reeds behind Kolumbe Island, but not her body. The coast-guards were asked to keep a watch. Once Ralph and I had to go up and look at a woman they'd found on the beach, but it wasn't Kate.

"No one had any idea what she did after she left the house. All Ralph could say was that on the last evening, she told him she'd cancelled her Hallowe'en party. From that small change of plan, people built up a crazy tower of rumour. Although Ralph said he believed she must be dead, the story got about she'd gone away with a man. There were friends, so-called, who were ready to name names. The Corbitts didn't go that far, but they did say they'd rather believe Kate had absconded with someone else's husband, than that she was dead. The papers ran the thing for all it was worth. Ralph was very bitter about it. He was a quiet man, as you know, and hated gossip, particularly when it buzzed round his own yard. He accused the Corbitts of spreading malicious rumours, and in no time there was a full-scale war between the two houses.

"The rest of the Crescent took sides, and then the whole town seemed to get involved. Things were said that couldn't be forgiven. The end of it was that Ralph dissolved his partnership with Sharvey, sold the town property, and moved out to the farm.

"Kolumbe had been badly neglected during the war and he

24

set himself to putting it right. He felt he owed that to you. Kate's share in Kolumbe was willed to you, and Deirdre's would be yours in time. I think out there Ralph felt close to them, and to old Sidney. In fact, all the people who meant anything much to him were associated with Kolumbe, and he was as happy there as he could be anywhere."

Evan stopped abruptly, looked at his watch and beckoned the Indian waiter across. There was so much I still wanted to ask him, but I could see the old sardonic impatience coming down over his face as I watched.

He paid the bill and I followed him out into the street. We tramped back to where I'd parked the Volvo. As he leaned down to open the door for me, I touched his wrist.

"Evan, one more question. What was wrong with Gretha Corbitt?"

"I never said anything about her."

"I know. That's why I ask."

He turned up his collar against the rain, and stood holding the lapels with both hands. "Gretha Corbitt was . . . I suppose they have some word for her . . . retarded, inadequate. A couple of centuries ago they'd have called her a witch."

"Ugly, you mean?"

"No, not at all. Fine silky brown hair that blew about, and huge green eyes with absolutely nothing behind them. Maybe Cassandra had eyes like that. You couldn't be sure what she saw, what she knew. And she had this hunger for attention, for affection, she responded to anyone who had time to spare for her. She adored Kate, because Kate would always turn aside from what she was doing, to talk or listen. After Kate died, Gretha was ill for months. That was the point when she became really disturbed. She was just eighteen, but she insisted on moving into a separate part of the house, the part the Corbitts used to call the garden flat. She refused to see anyone except her doctor, and pretty soon she refused to see even him. Over the years she grew more and more suspicious and hostile. She had bars fixed to all the windows, and fancy locks on all the doors, and let the hedges run wild. She hasn't left the Corbitt property for twenty-odd years."

"But if she was eighteen, a minor, why didn't they make her see a psychiatrist?"

Evan turned his face away so that I couldn't see his expression. "They feared her."

"Feared!"

"Lennie, you're too young to know what it is to look into the face of prophecy!" He seemed to pull himself together, and said in a quieter tone, "Gretha has a recognised form of mental disorder, a horror of the world, a mania to collect and hoard. She never throws away rubbish, except perishable things. She's kept every bottle and newspaper and piece of string that's come her way for two decades. At one time the Corbitts used to get into her apartment and clear it out, but now she prevents them from doing so. She allows them to cart stuff from the bottom of her garden, or from the stoep where she throws it. Nothing more."

"But that's crazy."

"If you like. I'm no longer sure in this day and age what's crazy and what's sane. Sane people pollute the sea and poison the earth, they turn flame-throwers on one another. Gretha is insane and lives her life as she wishes, harming nobody. Don't ask me to judge the Corbitts for not sending her to an asylum. Anyway, it's none of my affair. Goodbye, Lennie."

He waited for me to climb into the car and closed the door with an abrupt movement. I felt, as he went stumping off along the pavement, that he was separated from me not by yards, but by a distance of twenty years.

⑨ ⑨ ⑨

IV

L ATE THAT NIGHT I was still going over what Evan had told me. I felt he'd kept back part of the truth, perhaps to spare me, perhaps to spare himself. I felt Kate and my father had been very close to him, and there was a good deal of bitterness under his reticence.

I slept late next morning. After lunch I went to the City Library and checked the micro-file records of the evening and morning newspapers for October 1946, which was the month Kate Falconer vanished. Evan was right when he said there weren't many facts, but there was a whole stack of rumour and hearsay and unvoiced suspicion.

Kate left home on Friday, October 30th which was the night before Hallowe'en. She didn't tell anyone where she was going, or leave any instructions with the servants. She took a small overnight bag, so everyone assumed she was going to Kolumbe. The next day, Saturday, my father went fishing on the Bay. He came home late and asked my African nurse whether Miss Falconer had telephoned. When he was told she had not, he shrugged and said she would probably be back on Sunday night. It wasn't until Monday morning that he telephoned the farm and found she had not been seen at the farmhouse, at the shack, or in Kolumbe village.

He then reported the matter to the police, drove out to the farm, collected a search-party, and began to scour the land round the shack and the river. By mid-afternoon they had found Kate's dinghy. It seemed likely she'd taken it out to fish the water behind the island, been caught in the spate of the flood tide and overturned the boat.

From then on it was everyone's guessing-game. Within days the news columns reported Kate had been seen leaving Durban by train, by road, and in several different directions. A hobo on the docks had seen her board an American freighter, and a

27

salesman had watched her drive over the border into Swaziland in company with a man.

Questions were asked about her actions during the last days of her life. Why did she leave home without saying where she was going, why had Mr Ralph Bryant delayed so long before making enquiries, why had none of the Kolumbe Africans seen her on or near the river?

The answers can't have satisfied the average reader. Maybe Kate Falconer was an eccentric who went off without warning to outlandish places. Maybe the Africans at Kolumbe didn't see her because they thought the shack bewitched and never glanced that way. The chief question remained unanswered, "Where is Kate Falconer now?"

The Falconer case, they called it, and paragraphs about it appeared for weeks. I checked the files right through to the end of the year. Police in Europe, America and Australia were approached. They had no news of Kate. If she had left Africa, then she'd slipped through customs and passport controls that were particularly strict in a post-war world.

Legally, Kate was presumed to be alive. There was no body to be identified, no witness to give support to the theory of accidental drowning.

Yet by the end of November, it was clear that the newspapers accepted her death. On December 2nd a feature article discussed the legal aspects of the Falconer case. The point was made that it would be seven years before Kate was legally dead and the heirs could benefit. The story left a nasty taste. There was a pretty strong hint that Ralph Bryant was the loser, and serve him right.

In mid-December the evening paper announced that Ralph Finlay Bryant was taking legal action to prevent certain parties (not named) from spreading malicious rumours about his sister-in-law Katherine Falconer. At that stage the editors must have clamped down because I couldn't find any further reference either to Kate or to my father.

So Evan's anger and resentment were explained. Not only had he lost a close friend, but he'd seen her life made open day for scandal-mongers, and the blame for her death laid at my father's door; all of this without the smallest factual evidence.

There was a vindictiveness about the whole thing that was frightening. Why should a whole town turn its ill-will on a man who'd suffered a great deal and deserved sympathy and help? Surely that could only happen if someone took good care to make it happen?

Why should people like the Corbitts, who'd been friends of my aunt since childhood, suddenly spread the tale she'd absconded? What could they gain by gossipping?

Did the answer lie in Kate's own actions? Had she done something that jinxed them all?

There were several pictures of her in the files. One showed her sailing her boat, her hair blown across her head, her body braced against the tiller. She looked happy and without problems.

I went on turning the knob of the machine for some time. There was nothing more about the Falconer case, but I did find one small paragraph saying that the residents of Michael Crescent were forming an action committee to oppose the plan to build a shopping-centre on the property of the late Mr Sidney Falconer. The leader of the committee, it appeared, was Mrs Eleanor Sharvey.

My eyes and shoulders ached.

I switched off the magnifier and left the library and went out on to the steps of the City Hall. The traffic was making the usual five o'clock pretzels all round the memorial square. Beyond the bus queues, a hippie with shark-tooth beads on his chest was throwing corn for the pigeons.

It was funny but I couldn't get to the world out there. I was on the wrong side of a glass that stretched from earth to high heaven, and I couldn't get through. On my side it was 1946. Kate Falconer was lost and the whispers ran through town like sugar through a funnel.

Then the hippie threw a handful of corn and pigeons exploded against the sunlight, and the glass broke and I was back in my own skin.

29

I fetched the Volvo from the parkade and edged through the traffic-jams to the race course and then up the rising ground the first settlers called the Berea. At the crest of the ridge I turned right and drove to the very top of Peak Hill. From there I could get a good look at Michael Crescent.

⁓ ⁓ ⁓

V

THE LAND THERE is very steep. I parked the car by the roadside and walked down a lane between gardens until I reached the edge of the development site.

Evan had warned me to expect changes, but not as great as I saw. Last time I'd passed it, Peak Hill was covered with trees and shrubs and buildings. Now almost an entire block had been cleared. The land was stripped down to the bright red sub-soil, not a tree left, not a tussock of grass. The ground had been terraced and near the middle of the area they were already busy with the foundation levels of a mammoth apartment project. Skeleton roads threaded the complex, and a lot of yellow bull-dozers and cement-mixers were lined up next to a board that said "Another Hamilton Development".

They'd shaved Peak Hill to the bone. A whole cycle of plants, birds, animals and people had gone.

I sat down on a slab of rock and looked at the fall of the Berea, the sea turning a dusty pearl-rose, ships like sticks of charcoal with sparks of fire, and a burst of white sunlight that had got left behind on the clouds far out over the horizon. I looked at all this because I was avoiding looking at Michael Crescent.

But I did in the end.

I could see it quite plainly, stretched like a thirsty green tongue against the red earth on three sides of it. I could see the huge old flat-crown trees and flowering creepers, and the bits of white wall reflecting the sky colours. The shopping centre extended along most of the upper side of the green strip. That was where my family had lived. The centre had a flat roof and there were still a couple of cars parked there, a red Volkswagen and a maroon Mercedes. The steeple of St. Michael and All Angels seemed to have a bit of a slant. Perhaps they'd pull it down when they built the new church. I hoped they'd keep the old name. All Angels. All Saints, All Hallows. All Hallows Day was November 1st and Hallowe'en October 31st. Kate had cancelled the last Hallowe'en party.

While I was sitting there putting off thinking, I noticed someone else moving across Peak Hill. He was far away to my left and on a lower terrace. As I watched he scrambled up an earth cutting to my level, loped along for a while and then turned to face the sea. He had a camera with a bulky sort of lens attached to the front and he seemed to be taking pictures of Michael Crescent. There didn't seem to be much happening down there, except that the Mercedes was sliding down the ramp of the shopping centre and into Peak Road.

After a while the man came on towards me, his head bent as he detached the lens and put it away. When he was about fifty yards off, he looked up and saw me. He hesitated a moment and then hurried forward again as if he meant to skirt round and head for the crest of the hill.

"Hey!" I stood up and shouted without quite knowing why. He stopped and stared at me. He was an odd-looking guy, about twenty-six or -seven, with a narrow forehead, a thin hooked nose and a full mouth. There was a fringe of black beard round his jaw-line and his black hair was very neatly brushed back. With one gold ring in his ear he'd have done nicely for a cutlass-and-sabre epic.

"Well?" he said, giving me an impersonal eye.

"Are you designing the new church?" I said. It was the first thing that came into my head.

"No."

"Do you know who is?"

"I have no idea." He was almost past me now and gathering speed, but as he went he added, "Chopping and Spicer are the agents. They might be able to tell you."

"Thanks." I had this stupid, desperate feeling that I had to talk to him. I said in a loud unnatural voice, "Do you mind telling me why you were taking pictures of the Crescent?"

This time he spun right round and stared at me. His eyes were dark grey with glints in them like the flecks in granite.

"Give me one good reason," he said, "why I should answer your questions."

I thought a minute and then said, "It's important to me. The shopping centre was built on my grandfather's ground. I'm interested."

So, it seemed, was he. His face got a sort of intent look and he moved right up to lean against my slab of rock.

"I'm taking pictures of the entire site," he said. "The company wants to keep a record of each stage of development."

"So you're working for Chopping and Spicer?"

"Indirectly," he said. I got the impression this was a very indirect sort of man. Something about him permanently watchful and devious.

"And you?" he said, tilting his head sideways. "You live in Durban?"

"No, on a farm."

"Your grandfather was Mr Sidney Falconer?"

"That's right." He wasn't South African, I decided, but I wasn't sure if he was British or American or French. There was a sort of international flavour to the way he spoke, as if he'd never stayed in any place for long.

"You've been boning up on local history," I said, and he shook his head vaguely.

"Someone mentioned the name, I guess. Is it yours, too? Falconer?"

"No. I'm Florence Nightingale."

He gave a half-grin, then suddenly raised his camera and clicked it at me. "For my Crimean album. I'll send you a copy."

"Maybe it won't come out." It was a beautiful camera and he was obviously a professional. He gave me a cold look.

"My name is Dave Leatherhead, I'm staying at the Moncrieff Private Hotel and I don't have dark-room facilities in this town, so it may take a day or two to develop the pics. Where shall I send yours?"

I said nothing. I didn't want to give him my address and yet I felt I must keep track of him. Again his hard grey eyes scanned my face and as if he could see what I was thinking, he laughed. "It wouldn't be hard to trace you, you know. I know your grandfather's name, I have a photograph of you. Someone on the papers must know those Botticelli bones."

"A test of skill," I told him. He laughed again and slid the camera into his pocket, sketched a salute and set off, not up the hill this time, but down. I watched him run and leap down the red earth levels, diminishing at last to puppet size. He went up the steps at the side of the shopping centre, hopped into the Volkswagen and drove off.

The sun was gone behind the Berea and it was cold in the shadow. Yet I felt warm and exhilarated. I can't tell you why, except that everything, Mrs Hoburn's attack and my talk with Evan and this chance meeting with the man called Leatherhead, seemed to fit together, part of something that mattered to me. Two days ago I wouldn't have bothered my head about Kate Falconer. Now I felt the thread of my life caught up and twisted with hers, and more than that, the loom was moving, weaving, and the pattern running out for all to see.

I walked up the lane to the car and drove home with a thousand questions sparking in my mind.

Back at the flat I made myself some supper and ate it sitting in the bay window. When it was dark I went and 'phoned Polly in Port Elizabeth. We talked about her bowls tournament and the people she'd met and her match next day. I didn't tell her what I was going to do because I felt sure that would bring her back to Durban on the next Boeing. I'd made up my mind that first thing in the morning, I'd phone Nell Sharvey, and introduce myself.

    SS   *SS*   *SS*

VI

H E R   V O I C E   W A S beautiful, soft and yet sonorous, the sort that can fill a large room at any pitch. I said, in answer to her query, "This is Leonora Bryant, Mrs Sharvey. Deirdre Bryant's daughter."

There was a pause and I got a very strong impression that there was someone else with her, that she spoke to or glanced at. Then she said, "My dear, what a very pleasant surprise," and sounded as if she meant it.

"Could I meet you, and talk?"

"Of course. When would you like?"

"This morning?"

"This morning will be perfect. Come round any time you wish. We'll be down by the pool, I expect. Ask one of the servants to show you the way, or just follow the path from the front door through the rose-garden. If you want to swim, bring your things."

It was all too easy. Not many people want strangers to call on Saturday morning, particularly strangers from the embattled past.

At ten o'clock I left the Volvo in Peak Road which is wide and expensive, and walked round the corner into Michael

34

Crescent. The first thing that struck me was the stillness. Though the sun was warm, dew lay under the poplars that masked the churchyard. I followed a pavement edged with turf, past high white walls, trees, the same thicket of bamboo that Evan had mentioned. The green couldn't quite blot out the row of cars that glinted on the roof of the distant shopping centre, nor the raw red hill beyond. I noticed there was no access to the shops from the Crescent. The residents would have to take the long way round by Peak Road.

The Corbitts lived behind huge teak gates. One stood ajar and I stepped through. A drive wound away across more clipped turf, impossibly green for autumn. There was no bird song, and when I moved up the drive I saw why. There were at least six cats lolling about on the flags before the front door; a Burmese, two tabbies, a ginger, a Chinchilla, and a black tom with insolent eyes and big fat feet. He was a bird-eater if ever I saw one.

I stood and took in the house. The walls were plastered, smooth and warm as beeswax, the woodwork was darker honey, and there were wrought-iron balconies at the upper windows, very light and delicate in design. It had about as much in common with modern Africa as the Magnolia Waltz, and obviously cost a fortune to maintain; or rather, it looked that way as far as the hedge.

This hedge stuck out from the facade about three-quarters of the way along. It was an enormous slab of un-pruned bougainvillaea that sent up great shafts of blossom like the spines of a Disney dinosaur. And as if that wasn't enough, over the hedge hung trails of golden shower, and convolvulus, and potato creeper. There were birds in there, all right, finches and toppies and a collared sunbird. Beyond the hedge, I guessed, lay Gretha Corbitt's share of the property.

I turned away from that and took the path that wound round the right-hand side of the house, past roses and a border cleared for autumn planting, across a terrace to the swimming-pool.

This was as lush as the house. A bank of azaleas ran along the far side, and the change-rooms at the deep end were disguised as a Greek temple. From there to where I stood, a colonnade of pillars curved in a half-moon, enclosing a white marble patio. All the flowers near the pool were pink or white; begonia, camellia, white roses and daisies. Even the Alsatian that licked its paws in the sun, was white.

A man swam in the pool, racing under the surface of the water. At the deep end he did a somersault and streaked back. I watched him complete six lengths and was sure that the last four were exhibition stuff. Eventually he came to the side and pulled himself out and strolled towards me.

He was about fifty years old, with the swimmer's powerful sloping shoulders and thick thighs. There was too much flesh on him, but he looked hard and fit. He had the sort of black eyes that say they can get you into bed any time they please. I disliked him on sight.

"You must be Leonora Bryant." He smiled and flicked water from his hair. "I'm Derek Sharvey. Come and sit down."

I followed him to the patio, where there were wicker chairs round a lapis-lazuli mosaic table. Sharvey set a chair for me and flopped down in another. The Alsatian got up and slunk round to the far side of the pool.

"Nell's gone to see to tea," said my host. "She won't be long."

"It was kind of her to let me come."

"Nonsense. We're delighted to meet Deirdre's daughter. I courted your mother, once, you know. She'd have none of me."

A mark of good taste, I thought; and smiled at him.

"You don't resemble her, do you?"

"I'm supposed to take after Kate."

"So I hear." His chuckle was as insolent as his eyes. "Do you have her talent? At pottery, I mean?"

"Not yet."

"It'll come, it'll come. And how are things out at Kolumbe? Prosperous?"

"Fairly."

"Sugar's done well these past few years, but I suppose you've felt the drought?"

"The farm's all right. The sanctuary suffered. We can't irrigate down there."

"I suppose not. You're interested in birds? So am I, but not the feathered breeds. Birds, God help us! I don't see it. There's no money in a sanctuary."

36

"None," I agreed.

"So I can't get excited about it. Making money is my interest. Only thing I'm good at." He grinned at me.

"You swim well."

"Oh, I did, once. Now it's exercise to keep me fit for making money and love."

There was a certain fascination to him. You had to watch him, the way you have to watch a shark in a tank. "Tell me, Miss Bryant, what made you decide to look us up?"

I was ready for that one. "I'm writing a book, a biography of Kate Falconer. I'm tired of being saddled with an unsolved mystery, so I've decided to exploit it."

"Writing? That can be dangerous. Watch out for law-suits, my dear."

"I intend to. That's why I want to get my facts straight."

"Straight from the mules' mouths? Very sensible. What do you mean to ask me, for instance?"

"The reason you broke with my father."

"Umh." He leaned his head back and watched me under his lashes. "Good question. Your father was a dear chap, a good friend, but no businessman. That was the crux of it. I'm mercenary, he wasn't. Sometimes that's a good combination in partners, but it finished us. We couldn't agree on expansion targets. Ralph wouldn't grab opportunity even when it sat down in his lap. Yet he'd take risks in other ways. Oh yes. He'd put money on any outsider you cared to name. Ran himself into big trouble. He had to keep up that big house, the farm didn't pay, and your grandpa left most of the lolly to Kate. Something had to go and Ralph decided to sell out of the business and buzz off to Kolumbe. I didn't try to stop him. I always say, people do what they want to, in the end. So there were no hard feelings between Ralphie and me."

"There were hard feelings when Kate died, though, weren't there?"

Sharvey glanced towards the house. "Well, since you ask, things were never right after Deirdre died. The women started to fight, God knows why, and once that happens the men can just duck and pray. Fact is, Nell never got on with your father.

Thought he was too easy-going. When Kate did the vanishing act, Nell wanted to be up and doing, organising people. Ralph said it was no use, she was dead and buzzing about only attracted the crowds. He was right of course but there were plenty who said he just didn't care. He did the best thing, leaving Durban. I saw him quite often, lunch at the club or a round of golf when he was in town. We kept in touch."

He leaned over and took a pack of cigarettes from the table, offered it to me, lit his own and shook out the match, an expert pantomime of pre-occupation that he must have worked on for years, just as he'd worked on his attitude to Ralph and Kate. He had his story pat, and so would the rest of them. Yet underneath he was worried, excited, curious. The black eyes that saw so much had found something that couldn't be talked away.

Now he rubbed one hand across his stomach and gave me the big, avuncular smile. "Leonora, there's no doubt you'll get your kicks out of writing a book about Kate, but is it worth it? To begin with, they'll fight to keep it from being published. I wouldn't blame them. Feelings ran pretty high here, and I tell you frankly, I wouldn't like to go through it all again. But leave their feelings aside. What about you? I mean, do you really want to dig up all that muck?"

"I don't know," I said. "That's what I'm trying to find out."

"They'll try to stop you."

"Who's 'they'?"

"My family. Nell and Nick particularly." He moved his shoulders as if he were tired of the subject, tilted his head and blew smoke at the sky. His eyes focused on the hill behind the house and at once his earlier complacency returned. There was something childish in the man. He was like a child with a toy train, switching the points and crowing when the engine came in to the station.

I decided I wouldn't waste time checking on what he'd told me. Mr Clever Derek was much too fly to lie about facts that could be checked. But the facts weren't as important to me as the motives and sentiments and character of these people. Derek Sharvey's were written clearly in every line of his young-old face and well-preserved physique. Sharvey was fast and smooth and shallow as a puddle. No doubt he'd be a formidable business opponent but as a human being he was a pushover, because his vanity was so enormous he couldn't even see the effect he had on others.

"You'll be overshadowed," I said, and as his head came sharply round I added, "by the new buildings?"

"Oh, those? Yes. The area's zoned for flats now. One can't prevent it."

"And Michael Crescent? Do the residents have an agreement about selling?"

An extraordinary look crossed his face. Hate and resentment and a sort of glee as well. He said, "My dear child, the Corbitts and their ilk have no need for agreements. They know the right people. They have mystical powers. My wife for instance, she's drawn a magic circle round this house. Any speculator who dares to step over the line is immediately turned into a frog and fried in batter. How else do you think we keep our cats so sleek?"

"I thought they fed on birds," I said, and he shook his head.

"Fried frogs, from the enchanted palace."

His smile shifted past me. I turned my head. Not more than three yards away was a group of people; a tall woman in a green dress, a man in a wheelchair, and behind the chair a chunky guy with yellow-white hair and a very tanned skin. All three of them must have heard every word Sharvey said, but their fixed smiles showed they were determined to ignore him.

The woman moved forward. "Leonora! What a lovely surprise!"

I had the feeling this was the mis-statement of the year. I rose from my place and held out my hand. Sharvey laughed. On the far side of the swimming-pool the white Alsatian set up a loud, monotonous barking.

VII

I F T H E T A L L woman was making polite noises on one could hear them. She put her hand to her temple and said, "Cory, go and stop him!" The chunky man moved off round the pool and the Alsatian backed away, dancing, wheeling and roaring defiance. Sharvey laughed harder and the man in the wheelchair stared at him with contempt. The woman finally made herself heard.

"I'm Nell Sharvey, and this is my brother Nicholas."

He looked up at me without altering the position of his head. "How do you do? I'm sorry I can't shake hands with you. The wretched disease is anti-social." I saw that his hands lay twisted in his lap, the fingers swollen and gnarled as dahlia roots. His face was thin and heavily lined. Pain could have done it, although there was something about the droop of his mouth that made me think he might have earned some of the lines the easy way, in his wild and whirling youth. You could see he must have been attractive. The eyes he raised to mine were intelligent, but held no light, only an extreme weariness. It was the woman on my left who radiated vitality.

She had drawn up a chair and sat quietly, straight-backed, watching the thick-set man chase the Alsatian. The dull green colour of her dress reflected on the skin of her throat. Her face had a luminous pallor that was still perfectly healthy. The teeth that showed between her slightly parted lips were small, white and even. Her eyes were hazel, enormous under straight thin brows, and she had a pointed chin and a wide jaw. Her hair must once have been very fair. Fine as silk, it was brushed back from her forehead and then forward again under the ears. She made me think of Lombardy poplars. There was a grace and loneliness about her that hypnotised me.

"Tea's coming," she said, and smiled. "How like Kate you are, my dear, but easier to look at." Her gaze studied me calmly from head to toe. "Kate was very disturbing, you know. She had such eyes, like the sea on a hot afternoon, dark burning blue. Like that. And always restless, always moving. One felt she wanted to turn life upside down and shake the gold from its pockets. Are you like that? I hope not, for your own sake. It's a dangerous way to live."

Was it a warning? Nell's smile was gentle, almost languid, and yet I could feel the tension all about me. I said, "You must have thought it odd of me to 'phone as I did?"

"Oh no. I've been expecting you for some time. For years, in a sense."

"Saw you in her crystal ball," said Derek Sharvey, and his wife turned her quiet gaze on him.

"No. In the shape of events. Human nature is quite predictable. Something happens, we react. There was the piece in the *Chronicle*. You read it?"

"Yes," I said.

"And were prompted to enquire about us. To meet us. Well, it was bound to happen some day. Often I thought of writing and asking you to come. But we live a retired life. One puts things off and after a while they become difficult, and at last impossible."

A Zulu was coming across the terrace with a tea tray, and behind him stalked the black tom-cat. The tray was set down in the midst of us, and the cat took its place on the right of Nell Sharvey. She poured a saucer of milk for it and set it down, and then poured tea for us. Her hands moved slowly, gracefully. The fingers were long and strong as weeds under water. What she held she'd never let go. All the while, she talked in her beautiful voice.

"Do you know who was responsible for writing that article? No? A deliberate mischief-maker, I feel sure. Someone close to us, perhaps. Well, he'll find he's wasted his spite. The modern world has no time for the problems of the past. These days there is so much noise and sex and destruction that one's own troubles seem minimal. One has one's own security, one's own little castle as my husband pointed out. You have your sanctuary. We have this place. Your mother and your aunt knew it well. Of course it looked a bit different then. There was no

41

terrace, no swimming-pool. And some rather messy trees, mangoes and figs, that we took out. There was a swing over there, and we had a Shetland pony that bit people. Kate could handle him. She was good with animals, and birds. Have you the family trick?"

"I work with birds at Kolumbe. I'm doing a series of models of the water fowl and storks."

"Models? Like Kate? Of course, you've studied all these years. As children we fed the finches, put out crumbs and fat. Kate said if you behaved in the right way they would come to hand, but I never learned the knack. They never came to me, though I stood as still as stone."

"It's not just stillness. A stalking cat keeps very still. It's more something inside you. I don't know. Receptiveness? You have to project welcome and liking. Plenty of people can do it. St. Francis could, for one."

"Animal magnetism," said Nell. "Kate certainly had that. Everyone was drawn to her. Men especially."

The words carried no malice. Nell spoke as if she had planned exactly what she would say to me. I felt like a stick on a stream, being turned this way and that, carried steadily along. "Katharine," said the voice, "attracted men, and they attracted her. That was the root of the trouble. She was motivated by sex. I don't mean that harshly. She was not promiscuous as people said, but from the time she was sixteen she was always involved with some man or other. Often they made her very unhappy, but she couldn't live any other way. I never felt any doubt, when she disappeared, that she'd gone to a man. I was glad she'd left. She wasn't at all happy in Michael Crescent. Your father irritated her. It was an artificial arrangement, her living there. Kate wasn't the domesticated sort, not the sort to give up her work and her own way of life to look after a widower and a small baby. I told Ralph so, many times."

I had a pretty clear idea by now of the way everyone "told Ralph". He was a slow man, impractical, but not a weakling. He must have had a bellyful of their telling. But Nell's voice swept on and over my thoughts.

"Then Kate was in love. Those last few weeks you couldn't miss it. It was plain she was struggling with her conscience. She felt she had a duty to Ralph, but she wanted to break free. Ralph never saw that he was tying her down. In time it all became too much for her and she simply walked out. I still believe she went to a lover, but we shall never know the end of the story, because the accident intervened."

She hesitated, watching me, thumb and forefinger gently pinching her lower lip. Then suddenly she spoke with a new intensity. "We had to search for her, didn't we, Leonora, loving her we had to believe we might find her? You can't just sit back and say, 'she's dead, forget about her'? We may have been tactless but is tact the most important thing in the world? Afterwards, of course, when we knew Kate must be dead, we tried to approach Ralph, but he'd never forgive us. Never even talk to us. Life is . . . silly. There's far more silliness than tragedy. But the silliness destroys you just the same."

She turned her face away from me, and when she looked back I was startled to see her eyes were luminous with tears. "It was a bad time for us. Not just because of Kate, but because we were very hard up, and Nick was ill. He nearly died, the first year back from the war. Cory and I had to nurse him day and night. Every movement was agony for him, he carried pain-killing drugs everywhere. We gave up all social life. It was no good trying to keep up.

"Later, Nick got in touch with his old regiment. He needed an interest. You know the monument they unveiled last year? That's entirely due to Nick's efforts. He's collected nearly a quarter of a million rand, over the years. I don't want to bore you with things that can't interest you, but what I'm trying to say is that we built a life for ourselves, time slipped by, Ralph died and we lost track of all our old friends. I couldn't approach you. Your aunt Polly never held any brief for a Corbitt. By the time you were grown up and could make your own decisions, it seemed . . . well . . . cruel to seek you out. Better to let things go on as they were.

"But now . . ." she gave me a sudden brilliant smile . . . "now that we've met and talked, I hope you'll come and visit us often. Come and talk. We shall like that, it will be a reminder of Kate

43

and Deirdre and the happy times we had before the war. I hear you're using Kate's kilns again? Do tell me about your work, I want to hear all about you."

She nodded and smiled. In a moment I would have followed her into some conversational backwater, but I happened to look at Derek Sharvey. He was sitting with limbs spraddled, chin on chest, watching his wife with a sort of angry admiration.

So I didn't answer Nell's question. Instead I wedged myself more firmly into my chair and said, "I'd rather talk about Kate, Mrs Sharvey."

She looked both flustered and annoyed. Before she could speak, however, Nick Corbitt raised one of his twisted hands in a gentle but imperative gesture.

"One moment, Nell. There is something we should settle at once." He turned to me. "I would like you to tell me, Leonora, what you were doing up on Peak Hill yesterday evening?"

§ § §

VIII

IF HIS QUESTION startled me, it also startled the others. Nell and Derek Sharvey stared at Nick in blank shock. The calm, the sweet reasonableness around us, blew away like a dandelion clock.

"On Peak Hill," said Nell, swinging round at me, "you were on Peak Hill? Why?"

"I wanted to look at Michael Crescent," I said, and I could feel my face going red as fire.

"Why?" said Nell again.

"I wanted to see how far the development had gone."

"To the limit of human greed," said Nell in a harsh voice. "As far as it will go. They will not get the Crescent."

"How will you prevent them?"

"I will prevent them by holding what is mine," she said. "I will do what your father should have done. Sit tight."

"You always tried to prevent his selling the house, didn't you?"

"Yes, I did. He sold in a fit of spite, nothing more. To spite us."

She made a snapping movement of her long fingers. "Oh yes, he was very bitter, your father. He punished us for our mistake about Kate. Selling that land was the worst thing he could do to us, so he did it. Luckily we were able to prevent the supermarket having access to this road, and after that we were on guard. We have had a committee for twenty years. We've resisted every attack on the Crescent, and we shall continue to do so."

Nick glanced up at the hillside. "What protects us, Nell, isn't your committee, but the fact that that monstrosity up there has already destroyed this area. Our properties have dropped so much in value that no one wants to sell. If the Council re-zones Michael Crescent to allow more shops, prices will recover and these last houses will go, whatever you say. People can always find a way out of an agreement if the price is right."

Nell's lips folded fiercely, and her brother turned back to me. His voice was affable but his eyes were not. "There was a young man on the hill with you. He was taking photographs."

"He wasn't with me. I never saw him before in my life."

Nick raised his brows. His weariness had vanished entirely. He looked alert and somehow entertained, as if someone had shown him a diverting new game.

Derek Sharvey leaned forward in his chair. "What I'd like to know, Nick, is how you knew Leonora was on Peak Hill?"

"Cory saw her. She met the young man and they talked."

"Cory must have excellent eyesight."

"No, excellent binoculars."

"So he'd recognise the man again?"

"I don't think they'll meet, do you? It was no one we know."

45

Nick spoke with soft malice. "Unless, of course, it was some friend of yours?"

Sharvey's mouth drooped at the corners. He leaned back once more and drummed his fingers on the side of his chair.

"Leonora," Nell was apologetic, "you must think us very rude. It's this Peak Hill development. I'm afraid we have a thing about it. It's caused us untold misery. We've been pestered to sell, spied on, bullied, they've tried every legal and illegal trick to get us out."

"People have to live somewhere," muttered Sharvey, and she rounded on him.

"Much you care about people! You say that because you know it drives me mad!"

"Hush, Nell," said Nick. "We can't expect everyone to feel as we do."

"But why was that man taking photos? It's another trick, you'll see!"

"Perhaps, perhaps not. Leonora, could you see what exactly he took?"

"I think, the shopping centre."

"With a telescopic lens?"

"Or wide angle. I'm not sure."

"Then he probably got the whole Crescent. Did he tell you who he was working for?"

"No."

"Or his name?"

I lied. "I don't know it."

I'd had enough of them. They sat in this wonderful garden and breathed hate, and I felt it was a hate they'd shared for a long time. It held them together like lovers. I wanted to be out of the place, and I got to my feet, ready to say goodbye and good riddance, but I didn't quite make it.

It was the Alsatian that fixed me. It must have got away from the man called Cory and crept into the shrubbery behind me. As I stood up it sprang out and bounced at me with a shattering bark. I got such a fright that I lost my balance and caught hold of the edge of the mosaic table. The next moment the whole thing teetered sideways, and the heavy tray with the tea pot and

46

cups and God knows what else slithered off and crashed full on to Nick Corbitt's hands. He gave a scream of agony. Nell jumped up and rushed to him, lifted the tray and tossed it on to the grass. She slid her hand into Nick's jacket pocket and came up with a bottle of pills, shook one into her palm and tried to press it between his lips. He turned his head aside, moaning. "Quick," she said over her shoulder, "fetch Cory. Tell him to bring a syringe."

Sharvey took his time about getting up. He watched his wife for a moment and then turned to me. "I'll have to fetch his nanny for him. You'd better catch that bloody dog if you can, and shove it through Gretha's gate. If Nell gets hold of it, she'll kill it."

He loped off across the terrace. Nell Sharvey was cradling her brother against her, crooning to him. I went off to look for the Alsatian.

I X

IT'S AMAZING HOW many places there are for a dog to hide in a large garden. I moved away from the pool, peering under bushes and circling round flower-beds. I saw Cory Bergen come out of the house and run towards the group I'd left, and then a bank of shrubs hid them from view.

I found myself on a wide lawn studded with trees. Their mottled shade seemed somehow to increase the heat of the sun. It was absolutely still and quiet. I whistled and the sound was sucked into the spongy turf under my feet. Without meaning to, I began to hurry. I plunged along a path that seemed to lead to the house, and it led me into a little dell full of mole-runs and the stink of fungus. Doubling back, I tried again, and this time ran into a massive wall of creepers. For a moment I was ready to yell, then I realised what hedge this was and turned to the right and began to work my way along it. I came at last to a wooden door, unpainted but solid in the midst of a thicket of briars.

That's the way it happens, I thought. There's always a door to the enchanter's garden, and the poor yokel who finds it can choose: go through to a world of dangerous opportunity, or stay outside, safe and sorry for the rest of his days.

I touched the door with my fingertips and it swung back soundlessly . . . oil, I noted, and not magic. Beyond it lay long tangled grasses and weeds under neglected fruit trees. The branches were thick with birds, moving restlessly, silent and wary. I whistled to a band of toppies, they listened and then broke into a clinking, bubbling chatter. Finches bickered among the green peaches, and in the shadows just to my right, a woman laughed.

"Kate, they welcome you home. What did you bring us from Kolumbe?"

She was standing close under the hedge, but she stepped forward now, holding out both hands palm up, like a child. She was taller than Nell but had the same pale skin and pointed jaw-line. Her eyes were green instead of hazel, and I saw what Evan meant about them. They were blank yet expressive, like an empty sky that reflects light from beyond the horizon. Her brown hair hung in loose strands to her shoulders. She wore a white dress, rather crumpled, and white sandals with thick cork soles. Her legs and arms were thin and sunburned and scratched in places, as if she spent a lot of time burrowing through the briars.

"When you spoke to the toppies," she said, "I was sure." Her cold hands closed momentarily round my wrist. "Kate will come home, I always told them that."

"My name is . . ." I began, but she cut me short with a petulant shake of her head.

48

"Kate. All those people lied, you know. I wouldn't listen." A cloud troubled the smoothness of her forehead. "And then they said, 'She is not dead, but sleeping'."

She leaned past me and before I could stop her, pulled the garden door shut. I noticed that there was a new and efficient spring lock on our side.

"Come," she said, and went striding away up the pathway to the house. Halfway there, the white Alsatian tumbled out of the undergrowth and fawned on her. She pushed it away impatiently.

"Down, Lorca."

I followed her, stepping carefully, for the path was a tank-trap of holes and creepers. She led me round two sides of the house, past boarded windows and a sagging greenhouse, to a courtyard enclosed by high, glass-topped walls. In one of these was a hatch with a spring catch. This she opened, and lifted out a box of groceries. She closed the hatch again, and with the box on her hip, led me once more to the front of the building.

"That hatch," I said. "Does it go through to the supermarket?"

She gave me a look that was mischievous and perfectly sane. "I had it done. They were so angry. They cut off their noses to spite their faces, you see."

She ran up some steps to a small porch, and fitted an enormous key to a door as thick as a tombstone. It swung back and she stepped through, beckoning me after her. For a moment I hesitated and her voice called softly from the gloom, "It's all right, Kate can come."

I crossed my fingers and went.

Inside it was like a mad warehouse. There was space for the door to open and for an adult to move away from the door along a passage eighteen inches wide, but that was all. On either hand, from floor to ceiling of what must once have been a spacious hall, were stacks of boxes, bundles of newspaper, tangles of wood and metal and faded material.

Light filtered down from a globe high above me. When I lifted my head to look at it, I caught the glint of what I thought must

49

be fine wires, that ran like a spider's web across and across the piles of junk. Then I realised they were nylon fishing-line.

Beside me in the tunnel, Gretha Corbitt chuckled.

"It's quite safe. They're not set." She reached behind me and lifted a loop of line that hung free, stretched it across the doorway and secured it to a hook with one deft twist. "See?" she said.

I saw. Anyone coming over the threshold now would bring a ton of rubbish down on his head. The hall was one great booby-trap.

"It's bloody dangerous," I said. "You could be killed yourself." Her only answer was another chuckle. Her hand closed round my wrist and drew me on. I stumbled after her, along the hallway, up a staircase crammed with packing-cases. Every now and again I caught that gleam of nylon line, and felt sick.

We climbed the first flight, turned, climbed a second. Above us leaned vague outlines, staggering piles of paint tins, broken furniture, battered statues, an old tennis-net. Twice we crouched through archways that trembled as we passed. There was dust everywhere, and a dank smell. Ahead of us flitted the white ghost shape of Lorca.

And then suddenly we were in the clear, standing upright, before a plain white door. Gretha threw it open. We walked into a clean, bright, perfectly uncluttered kitchen. Sun poured through a window on to a scrubbed pinewood table, shining blue linoleum. Gretha dumped the box of groceries on the floor and hurried forward, beckoning me after.

The last room of all was enormous. I realised it must take up most of the top floor of the apartment. Perhaps it had once been Josh Corbitt's library, because at one end was a little gallery that had been turned into a bedroom; four-poster bed with lace bedspread, rosewood dressing-table, curtains of lacquered chintz. Everything was twenty years out of date, and looked set to last a life-time.

The main part of the floor-space was for living. Through an archway to my right I could see an ornate bath, teak-enclosed, with gilt taps. On the left were dining-table and chairs, and at the farthest end, a pair of divans and three easy-chairs covered in faded velvet. There was a fireplace there, with only one object on the mantel, a piece of pottery.

Gretha was rummaging through a cupboard. I moved slowly across the room to the fireplace. There were six big windows in the front façade, and across each ran thick steel bars. Otherwise, everything looked normal, comfortable and tidy.

On one side of the hearth was a big dog-basket, with a red blanket folded in the bottom. Bookcases along both walls. I glanced at the titles. *The Gum-Nut Babies.* Albert Camus. *These Old Shades. Zorba. Beautiful Joe.* Pasternak.

And the piece of pottery on the mantel was, as I'd known it would be, an example of the work of Kate Falconer. Early work, a coloured seine-fisherman. You could smell the rum on his breath.

I stood there looking at the room and thinking it was the home of a rational woman who liked things in apple-pie order. How did that fit with the mad jungle I'd just crossed? This side of the door lay summer and sanity. Beyond it was a world that was cold and insane. Gretha Corbitt had designed both.

She was beside me now, smiling, holding out a glass of home-made lemonade and a plate of macaroons. As I drank her eyes watched me eagerly.

"I remembered about Spanish limes," she said. "I cut the peel the way you like."

"When?" I said.

"This morning. I saw you walk up the drive. I sent Lorca. I knew you'd come back with him."

One part of me was sure I must put an end to pretence. Another part warned me to be quiet. I set down the empty glass and moved to a chair. Gretha sank down on to the hearth-rug and gave Lorca a biscuit, which he guzzled in one piece.

"There was a man," she said, "who told me you were dead. I never listened to him."

"Ralph Bryant?"

"Yes. I never listened. Then there was another man who took you away." She raised her thin brown arms. "He carried you off and took you away from me. I asked them about that man, but they wouldn't tell me. Do you remember his name?"

Her eyes lifted to mine with such sharp scrutiny that I flinched. "I forget," I said, and the answer seemed to satisfy her, for she nodded.

"How could you remember? You were asleep, poor Kate. All those years, asleep. I know."

"Who told you?"

"No one. I saw." She stared through and beyond me.

"Where?" I asked. She didn't seem to hear. She rocked back and forth, and her lips moved faintly.

"Hush," she said. "Say nothing. The Others will be angry."

"Was it a dream? Did you see me in a dream?"

She raised her hands, thin pointed fingers making a mask before her face. "Sleeping," she said. "Dreaming. Your face was pale and your hair shone. You were not dead but sleeping. I told them. Nell believed me. She said you had gone away with a man and left us. But that was a lie! A lie!"

"Why would Nell lie to you?"

Her head twisted round sharply. She said almost with surprise, "Nell does lie. You know that. But I knew you would never leave me, or the little baby. I said so and they were very angry. They shouted at me. But I never did what they wanted. I came here. I waited for you. Oh, such a long time. Sometimes it seemed like years." She sighed. "But now it's finished. You're home, you're back, my darling Kate. What will you do? Shall we have a party?"

"Perhaps. If you want."

"Yes! Yes, a Hallowe'en party, the way we used to. I kept the favours. I have them, I'll give them to you." Her face shone with laughter and she sprang to her feet.

"We'll ask everyone in the Crescent. Won't we? We'll order fireworks, boxes full, and sweep up all the leaves. Do you remember how we caught Nick? We told him if he walked backward up the stairs and looked over his shoulder in the looking-glass, he'd see his true love? But it was only a sheep's head from the kitchen. We put walnuts in the fire, do you remember, and Deirdre's broke but yours burned right through!"

She began to pace about the room, talking faster and faster, throwing out her arms in wild and sweeping movements. She spoke of her childhood, and sometimes it seemed as if the past were present in the room, and then again the present seemed to disintegrate before the flood of her speech. She swept me away with her to the Michael Crescent she'd known, so that I could hear the dead voices call and see the houses full of people and the lights streaming out. I was fascinated and a bit scared; because all the time I could feel, under the music of her voice, an undertone of dread. She seemed to clutch desperately at the ghosts she raised. Her gestures grew more and more distraught and uncertain, she was on the brink of hysteria. I got up from my chair and started towards her but she swung away with an angry jerk of her body. Then just as I was deciding I'd have to try the return journey through the house alone, the tirade ended. Gretha stood quietly at one of the windows, craned her neck, pointed a casual hand.

"He's down there, watching again."

"Who?"

"Cory. Come and see."

I went to the window. Leaning forward, I could look across the tangle of shrubs and an open terrace, to what must be the kitchen garden. A man stood there, staring up at Peak Hill.

"He's not watching us," I said.

"That's just his cleverness." Gretha pressed herself against the glass in an effort to see further. "He wants you to think he's doing something else, but really he's watching me. That's what they pay him for, that and looking after Nick."

She spun round to face me. "Never trust Cory. He's a wicked man. He tried to poison Lorca once, but I found the meat in time. I wrapped it up in a parcel and sent it to them. Do you know what I wrote on the box? For Killer Bergen. That's what his name used to be. He thinks if I don't have Lorca, he'll be able to get in here. Well, let him try. I'll crack him like a cockroach." She gave a sharp nod of satisfaction.

Now she turned briskly from the window and smiled at me. "The favours! I nearly forgot!"

She went to a tallboy and opened a drawer, took out a narrow box tied with ribbon. "Here. I kept them a secret. Nobody knows but us."

Inside the box was a nest of cottonwool on which lay a number of thin china discs. I lifted one free. It had a greenish, luminous glaze. One side was flat. On the other, in light relief, was a peacock with spread tail. It was very delicate, exact and beautiful. Down near the base of the disc was a tiny monogram. I wondered why Kate had bothered to sign it. Even in this bit of nonsense her style showed quite clearly.

"Where did you get them?" I said.

"Off your table. I knew you'd want to keep them, so I hid them away."

I retied the ribbon round the box and slipped it into my skirt pocket. It didn't show if I kept my arm at my side. I said, "I have to leave now, Gretha. But if you need me any time, I'll come. Can you send me a note or something?"

She nodded eagerly. "Where?"

I gave her the address of the flat, and then started to give the farm address, but she waved that aside. "I know Kolumbe. You'll come and see me again, soon?"

"Very soon."

She put out a hand and gave my wrist a little shake. "Don't forget. I'll take you back, now."

So once more she led me through the labyrinth. I found the second trip as scary as the first. When we reached the front porch the clothes were sticking to my back.

Lorca, who'd kept ahead all the way, shot into the undergrowth and began to dig furiously. Red dirt spattered us as we went down the front steps.

Gretha Corbitt bent to peer at the dog. "What is it, boy? Have you found a bone?" She raised her head and considered me gravely. "That's a problem, isn't it? What to do with the bones?" She began to chuckle, and suddenly my flesh crawled. It was at that moment, as I stood havering, that there came a banging on the gate, thumps and someone calling my name. "Leonora, are you all right?"

The change in the woman with me was terrifying. Her face

became a mask, wild and vengeful, the eyes blazing. She took one step along the path and stood listening, and then raised her own voice in a shrill and mocking cry.

"Leonora, Leonora, are you all right?"

The banging on the gate increased. Gretha swung towards me, arms raised. "Go on, go away. Do you think I don't know you? You'll not come into my house. Get away from here!"

I turned and bolted. I hit the gate and went through it in one leap, nearly knocking over Nell and Derek Sharvey on the other side. Sharvey slammed the gate behind me. Nell put out her arms, and I fell into them.

$$\text{\mancube} \quad \text{\mancube} \quad \text{\mancube}$$

X

"I SIMPLY CANNOT understand how it happened. That gate is always locked."

We were standing on the turn-around by the front door. The sun was high and the cats lolled full-length. "We were so worried about you," Nell said. "Gretha didn't scare you, did she? She can be very excitable at times."

"She's a nut case," muttered Sharvey.

"No, she's not." Nell sounded as if she'd said the same thing all too often. "Gretha is not mad, she merely lives in a child's world of fantasy."

"She looked after me very nicely," I said. "Gave me fresh lime juice and biscuits."

They were staring at me as if I'd used a four-letter word.

"Do you mean," said Derek, "that you went into the house with her?"

"Yes."

"But nobody has done that for years. I wonder ..." his sharp gaze ran over me without any bedroom hints, "did she mistake you for someone else?"

"She called me 'Kate'."

"I told you." Sharvey stabbed a finger at his wife and she nodded. For the first time there seemed to be concord between them.

"I feel I must explain," she said. "Gretha never accepted Kate's going. We tried to soften the blow, and Gretha blames us for that. She calls us liars, as a child would, not wanting to face the truth. Lately she's been restless and we've wondered whether, seeing your picture in the newspapers, some memory has been touched. Tell me, did she ask you to do anything for her? Post letters, or run errands?"

"No."

"And the house is quite tidy and clean?"

"Everything is ... very well organised." I don't know what made me guard my tongue. Perhaps a sort of feeling that to talk about Gretha's house would be like telling an adult where a child hides its treasures. Besides, I had my own questions to ask. "She manages very well," I said. "Groceries, books, everything she needs. So she must be well enough to handle her accounts?"

"Where money is concerned," said Sharvey, "she's as sharp as a needle."

"She is not insane," repeated his wife. "Not in the sense that she should be certified. When Kate died, Gretha developed a trick of make-believe. It's a way of defending herself against the cruelties of life." She gave me a faint smile. "She includes us among those, on occasion."

"I see. I'm sorry to have disturbed her, and I'm also terribly sorry about knocking over that tray. Is Mr Corbitt all right?"

"Yes. Cory gave him his injection. He's resting, but I'm sure he'd like to say goodbye to you."

She led the way through French doors into a large sunny room that was half study, half bedroom. The walls were hung with Army groups, guns, a regimental colour in a silk case. In a wing-chair sat Nick Corbitt, a rug over his knees. His eyes were dilated, I supposed from the injection. He moved his head and smiled at me.

"Ah, you're back from elfland?"

"Yes. Mr Corbitt, I'm sorry I was so clumsy. You must have been in agony."

"An accident, please forget it." He slid his swollen hands under the rug. "And is the mission completed? You found Lorca?"

"Yes, he's back with your sister."

"Good. All's well that ends well. You must come and see us again, very soon."

"Thank you."

Nick shifted his position slightly and the man Cory Bergen came silently from the back of the room.

"Cory, perhaps you'd walk Miss Bryant to the gate? Nell can stay with me."

I said goodbye to Nell and Nick. Derek Sharvey had disappeared. Cory ushered me from the room and we started down the drive.

The man was hardly a willing guide. His smooth, rocking gait kept him always a little ahead of me, and when I spoke his gaze never quite reached me, brushing past me with a sort of impatient contempt. He was ugly, too. His cropped yellow-white hair looked artificially bleached, until one saw that his short prickly eyelashes were the same colour. Every now and then his shoulders gave a slight forward twitch as if he found his coat irksome, and that was strange because by the cut of it, it must have cost a lot of money.

"You're not fond of animals, Mr Bergen?" I said. That got me a straight look at last. His eyes were small and piggy. I could see why Gretha had called him Killer Bergen. He looked as if he'd like to start on me.

"Does Lorca often cross into this part of the garden?"

"No." His voice was husky with venom. "The silly cow let it out. She knows we don't like dogs."

"She couldn't guess what would happen. The table was my fault."

"Some day I'll fix Lorca."

"I understand from Miss Corbitt that you've already tried. Didn't you drop poisoned meat for him?"

His lips curled back. "She said that? She's loony, they should lock her up. A loony woman."

I could feel my hands sweating. My dislike of him was as physical as nausea. I felt he was far less normal than the woman he'd just insulted. He was the sort who'd poison a dog and enjoy it. How did such a creature come to be living in a place like this, how did the Corbitts stand having him around?

I said deliberately, "I don't believe Miss Corbitt is crazy. I think she's frightened. She's also brave enough to do something about it."

He glanced at me under his lashes. "Such as?"

"Such as getting a good watch-dog."

Again he made that restless movement of the shoulders. "Steak," he said. "She gives it steak. A dog!"

"Well, that saves disposal problems. No bones in a steak."

"What's that supposed to mean?"

"Gretha told me," I watched him carefully, "that the problem was what to do with the bones."

For a moment he glared at me like a toad that's spotted an insect. Then he shrugged.

"Nobody knows what goes on in her head."

We reached the teak gates and he swung one open for me. I didn't trouble to thank him or say goodbye, and nor did he.

I looked back, though, when I reached the corner of Peak Road. The Crescent was deserted, the gates of the Corbitt house closed. I could see nothing of it above the trees. It might, like the enchanter's palace, have vanished into thin air.

℘ ℘ ℘

XI

THE FIRST THING I did when I got back to the flat was take a good look at the favours Gretha gave me. I took them all out of the box and spread them on the dining-table.

The work was very delicate. Kate must have used a jeweller's glass for some of the detail, and for the monogram, it was so tiny.

Each of the plaques illustrated a different bird. There was the peacock, a dove, a shrike, an owl, a raven, a pelican, a cuckoo, a mynah, a turkey, an ostrich, a skua and a black eagle.

I put them aside for closer study with a magnifying glass. I went and ate smorgasbord at a hotel on the sea-front and then went and lay on the beach. The surf was rough and dirty after the night's wind and rain, so there weren't many people about. I lay soaking up the sun, and the harsh cries of the gulls and terns seemed like the voices of the Corbitts and Cory Bergen.

Out of the heat-haze some thoughts began to emerge.

First point was, I'd walked into the Corbitt household at the peak of a crisis. I wasn't sure of the cause. It could be the article in the *Chronicle*. (Could one of them have sent it? Not Nell or Nick, probably, but Sharvey might have done it for spite, and Gretha from some crazy motive of her own. If she read Camus, she was literate all right.)

It could be the Peak Hill development that was upsetting them. Did they connect me with that, because I'd been seen on the site?

Anyway, whatever the cause, the Corbitts had a crisis, and by blundering in I'd made myself party to it.

Second point of interest was Cory Bergen. I couldn't make out what a creep like that was doing in that sort of stuffy, conservative household. He looked after Nick, yes. And I'd bet my last cent that Nick looked after him, or he wouldn't stay an hour.

Third point, Gretha herself. It might be that she was round

the twist, in which case she'd get caught in one of her own booby-traps and that would be that. But I had the oddest feeling about her craziness. I mean, I actually liked her. Nutty or not. And I wasn't afraid of her, not until that last moment, out in the garden, when she heard them calling me through the gate.

She'd sent Lorca out through the gate to attract my attention? Kate's attention? Had she really mistaken me for Kate? The way she'd watched me was strange. Almost as if she was testing me, seeing how mad I thought she was.

She'd wanted me to do something for her. Nell had guessed that.

So perhaps she was an embarrassing nut who spent her time flagging down strangers and telling them fairy-stories.

Only I wasn't a stranger, I was Lennie Bryant, a piece of her own past.

Not crazy, but not sane either? A mouthpiece of the gods, spilling oracles in wild phrases?

What the hell I was supposed to do about it, I'd no idea.

At four o'clock the warmth went out of the sun and I left the beach. I stopped on the way through town and bought a small magnifying-glass. Back at home I studied my china discs again. The result was very interesting indeed. What I'd taken to be Kate's monogram wasn't anything of the sort. There was a different set of initials on each piece. I got a pencil and paper and made a list. It went:

Raven	D.S.
Shrike	C.B.
Dove	G.C.
Owl	N.S.
Peacock	N.C.
Pelican	M.S.
Cuckoo	H.K.
Mynah	P.K.
Ostrich	J.D.
Skua	J.C.G.
Eagle	I.H.
Turkey	R.B.

I thought about that for some time, and then I went and 'phoned Evan Cruikshank. This time I caught him without having to chase all round the city.

"What d'yer want?" he said.

"Take me out to dinner, Evan, will you? I want to show you my pottery."

"Don't leer at me, girl. I'm old enough to be your grandfather. Where would you like to go?"

"Sea-foods," I said.

"Want me to call for you?"

"No. I'll meet you."

"All right then, the Swordfish, at seven. Don't wear one of those damn maxi-things, you hear?"

"Okay. Seven. Thanks grandpa."

I bathed and dressed ... in a coral silk sari that I thought dealt with the maxi barb ... and then went down to get the Volvo out of the garage.

I was thinking so hard about my list that I was half-way into the car before I saw the man standing on the far side. It was Dave Leatherhead. He was wearing a beautiful grey suit, an orange silk shirt, and shoes with buckles. He took an envelope from under his arm and waved it at me.

"Your photographs, Miss Bryant."

"Thank you."

"Aren't you going to congratulate me on my acumen? Took me less than half an hour to identify you."

"How?"

"The social page of a certain newspaper. One look at that long nose of yours, and the secret was out."

"Botticelli, you said yesterday." I couldn't resist looking at the picture. It was good. He'd given me two copies, one matt, one glossy. When I looked up again he was sitting in the passenger seat, grinning at me.

"Can I drop you somewhere?" I said. "Here, for instance?"

"I'm taking you out to dinner."

"I am already going out to dinner."

"Really?" He looked so disappointed I felt mean.

"Really."

"Oh well, serves me right, I should have 'phoned." He started to climb out again. It was then that it struck me that I was being a fool. The encounter on Peak Hill hadn't been chance. He'd been taking photos of Michael Crescent. He was part of the Corbitt crisis, and I wanted to know what part.

"Come too," I said.

"And the host will clap hands when he sees me?"

"He won't mind. He likes exotic fish. That shirt of yours is going to ring the full peal of bells."

"Take me to your leader," said Dave.

Ⓢ Ⓢ Ⓢ

XII

A s   i t   h a p p e n e d Evan didn't even notice the shirt because as soon as we stepped to our corner table in the Swordfish, Dave produced a bundle of photographs for Evan to look at.

They were pictures he'd taken up the East Coast of Africa. Fish, flowers, birds and now and again people. They were really fine pictures. I've seen thousands of bird photographs, and hardly anyone knows how to do them. The thing is to get the characteristic points showing clearly, with the flight or resting pose typical, and then you have to add beauty of composition and accurate colour. That's not easy, but Dave had the trick of it. I just gazed and gazed and then I asked if he had copies I could buy for the Kolumbe files.

"No need to talk of buying, I'll give them to you. I've plenty of spares."

"The Pel's fishing-owl," I said, "where did you get him?" The answer shook me.

"Kolumbe."

"My Kolumbe? When?"

"About a week back. That is a magnificent place you have there, Lennie, I'd say it's one of the best small reserves anywhere."

So then we all talked a great deal. Dave told us that in the past four years he'd made a number of trips round Africa. It dawned on my thick wits that he was either in the top photographic flight and earning packets, or he had private means, or both. He'd seen a lot of countries through the lens of his camera, not all of them lands of milk and honey, and he talked with interest about them. I still felt he was a hard case who'd do just what suited him, but I knew he wasn't just a society snap-shooter.

We went in to dinner, and, while we waited for the langoustines to be grilled, I said, "Isn't it time we talked about the Corbitts? It's what I came here for."

Evan looked quickly at Dave, and Dave at me. I said, "They spotted us up on Peak Hill yesterday."

"How do you know?" interrupted Evan. "My God, you didn't go to the Corbitts' house?"

"Yes, I did."

"You have neither shame nor grace, my girl. What do you mean, they spotted you on Peak Hill?"

I told him about going up to the site, meeting Dave, and how Cory Bergen had seen us through binoculars. "I think," I added, "they believe Dave is working for the development corporation and wants to buy up Michael Crescent."

"Do they now," said Dave. "What did you tell them?"

"Nothing. I didn't discuss you, or mention your name."

"Thanks."

I was about to ask him exactly what he was doing on the site, but Evan was leaning forward with an air of great impatience. "What else? What else did the Corbitts say?"

I told them about my conversation with Derek and Nell Sharvey, and the incident of the tea tray, but I didn't tell about

63

going into Gretha's flat, because by that point I was beginning to scare myself. It's funny how you think about an experience and it seems okay but then you tell it aloud and it sounds downright sinister. So I just let them understand I'd taken Lorca back to Gretha's door and spoken to her. Even then, they looked at me in a very old-fashioned way.

"It seems," Evan said, "as if that piece in the *Chronicle* was deliberately inspired. I made a few enquiries this morning. It didn't come from the Peak Hill Development Company, nor from the agents, Chopping and Spicer. That means it wasn't straightforward publicity promotion. I went over and talked to the Property Editor. He tells me he's been on leave for two weeks and the story went in while he was away. What happened was, the underling left in charge found a typed draft of the story in his In-tray. He should have checked the source, but he assumed it came from the Features Editor, thought it made a good human-interest angle, and used it. Nobody knows how the draft was planted. It might have come by post, or by hand. Thing is, who wanted to drag up the old scandals? Not the Corbitts, that's certain." His eyes went thoughtfully to Dave, who looked startled.

"I didn't send it. I don't know one thing about it, I don't know the Corbitts and I'm definitely not trying to get possession of their strip of mortal earth."

"Then why were you on Peak Hill, taking pictures?"

"I was commissioned to do so."

"By?"

"I'm not prepared to discuss that. It has nothing to do with the Corbitt family." Or you, is what he meant.

Evan nodded. "Speaking of which, Lennie, did they advance any theory about the article in the paper?"

"None. They're puzzled and anxious. Derek Sharvey might have fixed it. Any mention of the Michael Crescent property riles his wife, and he hates her enough to get a kick out of that. But I don't think the person who sent that note to the *Chronicle* was interested in property. I think he was interested in Kate Falconer."

"Why?"

"I don't know, Evan, but I've got a nasty cold feeling in my stomach." I met his beady stare. "Was there ever a rumour that Kate Falconer was murdered?"

"For God's sake!" Evan looked absolutely horrified. "Whatever put that in your head?"

"Gretha. When I was talking to her she seemed to be . . . not exactly hinting . . . but giving out a sort of terror. As if she was trying to keep herself from remembering something terrible. It struck me that she may be the reason the Corbitts don't go out in the world any more. I mean, if Gretha harmed Kate in some way?"

"My dear child, you're raving. Gretha adored Kate."

"I know she did. And she was an unbalanced teenager when Kate decided to leave Durban. Don't you see, it fits? Kate suddenly makes up her mind to go away. Tells my father she's cancelling the Hallowe'en revels. Walks out of the house and goes next door to tell Gretha. Gretha becomes jealous, excited, strikes out at Kate. It could have happened."

"And the Corbitts buried the body in the basement, I suppose? Oh, don't make big eyes at me, Lennie. Just to bring you back to earth, let me tell you that after Kate vanished the police checked every inch of Michael Crescent. They would certainly have known about any new graves on the Corbitt ground. Stop imagining things." He paused while a waiter refilled our wineglasses and then tapped the table in front of me. "Imagination is a good servant and a dangerous master. Look where it got Gretha."

"All I'm saying is that something must have happened to send Gretha off her rocker."

"Something did. Kate went away. You must understand that to someone like Gretha, who is mentally a child, the intolerable thing is to be deserted. She feels that Kate deserted her, she is told by her relations that she was deserted because Kate preferred another person. That is something Gretha cannot and will not accept. So she hangs a veil of fantasy between herself and the truth. The people who persist in trying to break the veil become her enemies. She builds physical walls to keep them away from her. Within the walls, she can continue to live a life of fiction. Kate is alive,

65

sleeping somewhere. She will wake up and return, one day. That's the explanation of her wild talk, believe me."

"The trouble is, Evan, she's not all that crazy. I mean, most of the time I was with her I believed her. I liked her. I think she has the truth locked up in her brain and half wants to tell it and half doesn't. She's terrified that if she tells, something will happen to her."

"Terrified of her own relations?"

"No. I don't think she's afraid of them, but she's scared of someone. People she calls The Others."

"Crazy," said Evan. "I'm telling you, Lennie . . ."

"No, wait. Look at it another way. Someone sent a note to the *Chronicle* that sparked off a story mentioning Kate Falconer. Right?"

"Yes, but . . ."

"That someone is no friend to the Corbitts?"

"Agreed."

"Gretha might have sent it."

"Extremely unlikely."

"But if she didn't send it, she certainly read it. The flat is lousy with newspapers. She reads *Zorba* and *Zhivago*, she can read a column of newsprint."

"So?"

"So she knows who sent the story in. Or guesses. One of The Others. That frightens her so much she half-tells me, but changes her mind at the last minute."

"This is just speculation, Lennie."

"No, it isn't. Gretha gave me something that supports what I've said. A box of Hallowe'en favours. Favours made by Kate Falconer, I think for the last party that never came off. Each one of those favours is initialled. In other words, each one was meant for a guest at the party. Here's the list I've made, with the device shown on each favour, and the initials alongside.

I held the paper out and Evan spread it on the table so he and Dave could read it. After a while, Evan grunted.

"Raven, D.S., Derek Sharvey. Shrike, C.B., Cory Bergen. Dove, G.C., Gretha Corbitt. Owl, N.S., Nell Sharvey.

Peacock, N.C., Nick Corbitt. Turkey, R.B., Ralph Bryant. Doesn't take genius to work it out, they were her friends, they went to all her Hallowe'en nights."

"I'm not concerned with them."

"What then? These others?"

"Precisely, you said it, The Others. The people Gretha's afraid of. The people who know how Kate Falconer died."

"Lennie." Evan sounded on the edge of panic. "You are to stop this nonsense. And don't imagine that I shall allow you to go about town chasing up all the people with those initials, making a fool of yourself and upsetting ordinary decent citizens, because I shan't. Nobody will be able to tell you anything about those ciphers. Nobody at all."

"There you're wrong." Dave handed the list back to me with a faint smile. "I think I can help with one. The Skua, J.C.G. That to me means Jean-Charles Greco. Want to hear about it?"

⑨⑨⑨⑨

XIII

"NOT IN HERE," said Evan with decision. "My God, what have I done to merit this? Outside, both of you. We'll take coffee in what fresh air remains to us."

We went out on the terrace. Eleven stories down on the Snell Parade the municipality had done its thing with lights and sideshows; the sea beyond had a brownish, tired look.

"So who's this Greco?" said Evan. Dave turned from the railing and sat at the table.

"Jean-Charles Greco is the name of a very rich bastard. He's half French and half Turkish. His sphere of operations is Asia-Minor, Southern Europe and the Americas. Jean-Charles has had five wives, and every last one of them was so glad to be rid of him that she accepted a pittance in alimony. His money comes from small-arms sold to small-time revolutionaries, barter in phoney mineral-rights, and an international ring of faith-healers who act as cover-men for the drug-trade. Greco has never been convicted on any charge, nor detected in any strictly honest proposition. He dislikes being crossed. The story goes that he once dealt with a man who crossed him, by having him dropped from an aircraft into a lake full of crocodiles. Myself I don't think he'd have wasted the high octane. He never forgives an injury and will wait years to pay it back. He's a big spender and an even bigger taker.

"He made his first million appropriating the art treasures of anti-Fascists in Spain and Italy. Then he shifted to Germany. When the Nazi regime fell, Greco was just as quick to loot their lockers. All grist to his mill."

"You make him sound irresistible," murmured Evan.

"Oddly enough, to certain people, he is. My mother was one of them, although I'm glad to say Greco was not my father."

Evan ignored that angle. "Kate would never have been drawn to such a man."

"Can you be sure? There's a snake park down on the Parade there, full of reptiles. People pay to go and look at them."

"Yes, but they don't want to take them home."

"You say Kate liked to take risks. Well, Greco was King Cobra, a real challenge to any snake-charmer."

"What does he look like?" I said.

"Tallish, graceful, fawn-coloured. Some people have said he's of mixed blood, but that's not so. He's pure Mediterranean. Oval face with light-brown eyes, skin, and hair. He looks at you as if he's half-asleep, but don't ever make that error. He likes silk fabrics and cheap strong cheroots and he carries a tiger-eye stone as a good-luck piece. His voice is sort of greenish-gold, like diesel oil. He has a thing about washing."

"Doesn't, you mean?"

"Does, to excess. First thing he looks at in any place he stays, is the bathroom. The only time I ever heard him raise his voice was when someone got knifed at one of his parties and bled into the swimming-pool. He's a very fastidious man."

"Does he have any good points, besides cleanliness?"

"Well, he pays his debts, cash on the nail. He tells very good jokes in any accent you care to name. He speaks six languages well and several more intelligibly. He's a patron of the arts. The women say he's good in bed. He drives a Porsche like a pro. He can't be frightened. People who try to scare him tickle his sense of the ridiculous. The closer a man gets to killing Greco, the bigger the wreath Greco sends to the guy's funeral. I'm told he doesn't go much for violence these days, though. Says technology and electronics are the big thing in his field of operations. So the Greco of the 'seventies, I don't know much about."

"Why would a man like that," I said, "come to a small town like Durban? Why Africa, come to that?"

Dave shrugged. "After the war. Legend tells us that in 1944 the boy had to get out of Europe fast, because his war effort had been strictly for Greco and everyone wanted him, the Allies, the Maquis, the Greeks and the Italians. He slipped out via Casablanca and points south, making a few useful contacts en route—the Greco guns made a lot of noise in the Algerian thing later on.

"But he probably needed a place to shelter until the shouting died down. He'd have had jewels or heroin or information he wanted to turn into sterling, and South Africa was a quiet place to do it. But I can't tell you why he was invited to your aunt Kate's party. One thing is sure. If he accepted, then there was something in it for him, the chance of a business deal, or a crack at a beautiful woman."

Evan said flatly, "Kate would never have invited him. She was eccentric, but not that eccentric."

"Well, maybe she didn't know him. Maybe one of her friends got him the invitation."

"Who'd introduce a gangster to his home circle?"

I said, "Derek Sharvey," and Evan blinked and sat back in his chair.

"Sharvey's not that unprincipled."

"No," said Dave, "but who knows if Sharvey knew Greco's background. Greco would wipe his shoes on his old grandma if it suited him, but no one would see him do it."

"You know him pretty well," I said, and he gave me a tired glance.

"I spent my formative years in Greco's ambit. Fourteen years ago I cleared out. I hope never to set eyes on him again."

"Nevertheless," Evan said quietly, "it is a coincidence that Greco's step-son should turn up on Peak Hill in 1970 and take photographs of the houses Greco visited in 1946. One can't help wondering if Greco is interested in the area. You could be his agent."

Dave made an impatient gesture. "I told you, I haven't seen Greco in years. I wouldn't work for him if he was the last man alive. And he wouldn't touch real estate. It's too respectable, for one thing, and for another it's earth. Earth is dirt to Greco, something you have to wash off as fast as possible. Someone did him down over a piece of land, once, and he's never liked touching it since."

"Perhaps the land was in Michael Crescent."

"No. It was a corner site in the San Francisco graveyard where he wanted to bury his mother. It was sold to a Chinese who worked the Fa Fee racket. Greco's never liked land or chop suey since."

There was a sharp edge to Dave's smile that made me feel close to him. Nobody ever escapes his own childhood, I've learned that and it makes me sorry for anyone who's still running. But Evan never feels sorry for anyone, and now he leaned forward and watched Dave as if he had him in a specimen tank.

"Tell me, Mr Leatherhead, when did Greco marry your mother?"

"When I was four. In 1947."

"Where?"

"Montreal."

"So the marriage took place a few months after Kate disappeared." He brooded a moment, then said. "If Greco was the man in her life, if she went off with him, then it explains why Ralph didn't want the affair publicised."

I protested, "You said yourself she'd never even speak to a character like that."

"I don't want to think so. But apparently he was clever and plausible. And Dave's right about the element of risk. Kate enjoyed that. You see, Lennie, I loved Kate but I didn't always find her wise, or estimable. She did things because it amused her to do them. For kicks, you'd say. And she could be an awful fool. If she went off with Greco, it explains a number of things; Ralph's delay in raising the alarm, and her own mood during those last few weeks, excited one moment and depressed the next." Evan brooded, and sighed. "One thing I've always been sure of. On October 30th she came to some decision, and told Ralph about it. I know, because I was there.

"There were quite a few of us up at Ralph's that night, for drinks. Sharvey was there, and Nell and Nick and several others. It was one of those affairs when people come and go all the time. There were groups in the living-rooms and out on the terrace, everybody was having a good time but Kate herself was very quiet. I asked her if she was feeling all right and she said, 'Fine, but I have something boring and unpleasant to do and that makes me restless.' I asked if I could help, and she just shook her head and said, 'It's my problem, Evan darling, and it'll soon be solved, you mustn't worry.' Later I walked through to the drawing-room and she was there, talking to Ralph. They were going at each other hammer and tongs, not a quarrel exactly, but certainly a heated argument. Ralph told her she must 'observe the limits of good sense', and she laughed. Good sense never meant a damn to her, her life was governed by intense feelings, not reason. So then Ralph said they must both think of the child, and Kate put her head on one side and smiled at him. I remember just how she looked. Her red hair was shining in the light and it was exactly the colour of the sherry in her glass. She said, 'Indeed yes, Ralph, let's both of us think of the child. My advice to you is, do what Deirdre would have wanted for Lennie. It's her heritage, you must hang on to it somehow.' Ralph didn't answer at once because he'd seen me standing in the doorway. He just nodded, and said 'Very well, Kate.'

"She turned away at once and went towards the verandah. Ralph called after her, 'Where are you going?' but she just raised a hand as if to say, 'I'll be back in a moment.' I saw her walk along the terrace; and then she must have gone straight back to her room and collected a few things in an overnight bag, and left the house." Evan paused. "I never saw her again. At the inquest, I said I'd heard them arguing about the sale of the house. It corroborated Ralph's statement. It never struck me they were discussing more than one subject, that he could have been warning her against her own indiscretions. But it all fits, it makes sense. Ralph knew Greco, knew his reputation, and therefore didn't want it said Kate had gone off with him. The Corbitts, not knowing of Greco, didn't have the same inhibitions."

"They must have known people would start putting names to the mystery man," I said. Evan gave me a thoughtful look.

"I'm sure they did. But I think they had another name in mind than Greco's; a name that wouldn't excite any scandal, only sympathy." He reached over and picked up the list of names I'd left on the table.

"This one," he said. "The Ostrich, initials J.D. I believe that means Johan Dessels. Everyone in town knew he'd been after Kate for years."

$$\textit{\textcyr{5}} \quad \textit{\textcyr{5}} \quad \textit{\textcyr{5}}$$

XIV

"DESSELS THE BIOLOGIST?"

I was really startled. Johan Dessels is so high up in the world of science that you need an oxygen mask to talk to him, and I couldn't imagine him being part of any love affair, let alone one that turned into a public scandal.

Evan nodded, and then as if he wanted to play for time, sent for more coffee and brandies. When the order came he still didn't seem to know where to start but sat fiddling with his glass for some moments.

"I never could stand Dessels," he said at last, "so you can take what I say as biased evidence. He and I never got on. He's the most brilliant man, for his field, in the southern hemisphere, his written works are a significant contribution both to science and literature, his sacrifices in the personal sense have been immense, and I plain don't like him. Perhaps it's the dislike of the gabster for the strong silent man. Dessels is so bloody reserved I suspect him of monumental selfishness. If a man is too shy to sit and chat to an old man dying of throat cancer, as Sid Falconer was, then that shyness is itself a disease. Dessels didn't like people. He said so. He avoided human contact, he despised casual acquaintances.

"Yet he wasn't a cold man. His love for Kate was just the reverse, passionate and extreme. He is an extreme sort of man, in his own way. You want to see him fighting for some scrawny patch of desert or veld he wants to preserve. That was the interest he shared with Kate, an emotional kinship with the soil and the animals and birds that live off it.

"You say that Greco thought of earth as dirt. To Dessels it's holy, the basis of life in the most literal sense. I suppose it was his farming ancestry. He always showed the sort of land hunger one associates with a primitive rather than with a doctor of science. His father owned a couple of farms near Kolumbe, but sold them later and went to grow oranges up Muden way. One of the sons kept prize Guernseys at Cato Ridge.

"Johan knew Kate from childhood, and shared her feeling for Kolumbe, both the farm and the sanctuary. He helped her in her fight to protect the estuary from industrial poachers. Later on Kate went with him on journeys across Africa. The Etosha Pan, the Kalahari, the Rift Valley. They enjoyed kicking off civilisation. Kate could live sparsely for long periods. She told me once the only place worth living in was a place where one could be lost without trace. Prophetic, if you like.

"People said she and Dessels were lovers. They probably were for a time. But I'm sure Kate never thought of marrying him. Oddly enough, it was the very thing that brought them together ... Kolumbe ... that finally drove them apart. Dessels helped her to create the finest bird sanctuary in Africa, and then grew jealous of it. He saw it as his chief rival. He came to hate it and fear it.

"In the last year of her life they quarrelled often. She'd refuse to see him because of the way he raged at her. He'd run home to mother and stay away for days. Then back he'd come to haunt the house until Kate agreed to see him, and the whole cycle would start again. It was dreadfully sordid to see how abject he could be. I feel the same way about circus animals. But feeling sorry for him didn't make me like him.

"You know, when Kate died, Johan never came to see Ralph, never wrote to any one of us. He turned his back on everything that was associated with her and cleared off to Central Africa. He's been a nomad ever since. Never married, never bought a stick nor stone nor an acre of land. From time to time he'll come to town, attend to business, buy new equipment, publish a paper or address a conference. When he appears, we do our share of crawling. His knowledge is formidable. So is his loneliness. He's one of the greatest biologists of our era and I'll bet that at this moment no one knows where he is. Tanzania, Zurich, the moon. Or dining here at this hotel."

"Isn't there any way of tracing him through the scientific societies?"

74

"No. He leaves no address. He doesn't want to be found. One can only respect his wish."

Evan gave me such a severe look that I merely nodded. Soon after that I said I was tired and we broke the party up. It was only when I was driving Dave home that he showed me he was a hard man to fool. He said, "You're going to try and find her, aren't you?"

I said, "Who?" as innocently as I could.

"Johan Dessels' mother."

I said nothing, and Dave mused, "It figures. Evan said he ran to mother when Kate bitched him. A man like that would have a Ma in the background, devoted and cannibalistic. Where will you start looking?"

"North Coast," I said. "If they farmed at Kolumbe once, chances are the old lady's gone back that way."

"Dessels is a common name."

"I'll 'phone the stationmaster at Kolumbe. He's a thousand years old and remembers everyone's first name."

"If you find where she lives, I'll come with you. You mustn't go alone."

I thought about that. I didn't trust Dave Leatherhead. He knew a lot more than he was telling. But he also knew things I wanted to prise out of him. For instance, he'd been out at Kolumbe himself, last week, photographing my Pel's Fishing-owl. That was just a few days after the piece appeared in the *Chronicle*. And a short while after that again, he appears on Peak Hill, clicking away at the Crescent. Now he wanted to come and look for Mrs Dessels.

Well, let it play that way. If Dave was on the side of Michael and All Angels, it would be nice to have his company in case of trouble. If he was for the devil, then perhaps he'd take me to his leader.

"If I find anything," I said, "I'll let you know."

🔊 🔊 🔊

XV

W HEN I REACHED home I didn't go straight to bed but changed into a wrap and settled down in an armchair to sort out my ideas. Up till then I hadn't troubled to think where events were taking me. I'd told myself that any time I chose, I could forget the Corbitts and go home to Kolumbe. Now I saw that wasn't true. I was as much a victim of circumstances as the rest of the people in Michael Crescent. I was being dragged along by my Falconer nose.

That frightened me. Once when I was a child I walked on a lonely beach, and there was this old bottle lying in the dunes and the wind blew across it and made a constant, mindless sobbing. I never want anyone playing tunes on my empty life.

Another thing that struck me was that whoever wrote to the *Chronicle* didn't start anything new. The Peak Hill project, the Michael Crescent mob, the Kate Falconer case, were old drama. Apparently it amused some kinky mind to stage a revival and invite certain people to be present. I happened to be one of them, but my absence or presence wasn't going to stop the play. The curtain was up and the characters coming on stage.

They were a pretty mixed bunch. That they had always been. What did Jean-Charles Greco ever have in common with ex-hero Nick Corbitt? Or Johan Dessels with Cory Bergen? Yet Kate had planned to bring them together at a party, and on Hallowe'en, the witches' night when there's no more Christian charity abroad than you'll find in the hollow head of a pumpkin.

Had that party been one of the risks that Kate liked to take? I felt more and more certain that one of the people invited to it was involved in my aunt's disappearance.

I drew out the list, and studied it again. Of the twelve sets of initials, we'd now put names to eight. The four remaining were:

Pelican   M.S.
Cuckoo   H.K.

76

Mynah   P.K.
Eagle   I.H.

Now I thought about it, the birds chosen for the first eight had been apt. Derek Sharvey was the Raven, which happens to be a talker and scavenger as well as a fine dark fellow. The Shrike was Cory Bergen, the Dove Gretha Corbitt. Peacock was Nick. Well, his beauty hadn't survived the war, but his pride certainly had. Ostrich? Johan Dessels was the bird without wings, that inhabits the dry lands, and survives by its ability to run very fast from any pursuer. Nell Sharvey was the Owl, symbolic of wisdom, power and magic. Also in its minor way, a bird of prey. The Skua was Greco, and a Skua looks small and smooth, but challenge it and it becomes a vicious and vindictive fighter.

How I'd discover the identities of the final four, I had no idea.

I sat in my armchair for a long time, and then suddenly a plan came to me that made instant appeal, because it would put us on the attack instead of the defence. I fetched pencil and paper and began to draft an advertisement for the leader page of the *Chronicle*. After several tries I got it as I wanted it.

KOLUMBE QUIZ

PRIZE-WINNERS

R100

is awarded to

PELICAN . . . . . (M.S.)
CUCKOO . . . . . (H.K.)
MYNAH . . . . . . (P.K.)
EAGLE . . . . . . (I.H.)

Prize money will be
distributed on
application to

Box N. XYZ, *Chronicle*.

77

Next morning at eight I took in my draft. I had to convince the clerk at the acceptance desk that I wasn't running a lottery or sweepstake, and the prizes advertised were awarded on skill alone. That was true. It was going to take skill for anyone to chisel a single cent out of me. I was allocated a box number and told to expect replies from the following morning.

From the *Chronicle* office, I went to the Central Post Office. I looked up the number for Kolumbe Station and put a personal service call through to Mr Venter, the stationmaster. It took ten minutes of talk, but in the end he gave me the initials of every Dessel known to him. Old Mrs Dessels, thank God, had an ace collection of names. Christina Wilhelmina van Schoenwinkel Dessels. She was, Mr Venter let on, the daughter of a Boer General, and wrote poetry. He didn't know where she was living now. I thanked him and rang off.

There was no C. W. van S. Dessels listed in the Natal telephone directory for Durban and district. I ploughed through the north coast villages. Nothing for Kolumbe, Umhlali, Salt Rock, Ballito Bay or La Gratitude. Nothing for Tongaat. I could have gone on looking under every heading in the book, but I had this conviction Mrs Dessels would be somewhere near Kolumbe. Probably not on the telephone? I started listing the numbers of the main trading stores in each village. I knew a lot of the owners, and the owner of a backveld store knows everyone in his district, better than any postmaster or police sergeant.

At La Gratitude I struck lucky. Mr Moolla, who's a great gossip, told me that a Mrs Dessels with those initials owned a cottage on the beach about ten miles north of the village. She had no telephone and hardly ever came into the store. A very quiet lady.

More thanks, and I set off for the flat.

I wrote Mrs Dessels a very polite letter explaining that I was Leonora Bryant whose parents had farmed next to her husband at Kolumbe. I asked if I could call in and see her within the next day or two. I didn't give reasons. I addressed the letter to P.O. La Gratitude and expressed it. She would have it within twenty-four hours if she collected her post regularly, but not until after my advertisement appeared in the *Chronicle*. She might of course be a black-stocking Calvinist who never read the English-language press.

I sat back to await results.

Monday was blank. No replies. Tuesday started out a dud. Mrs Dessels didn't 'phone. There were some replies in my box at the newspaper office, but none of them helped. The one I liked best informed me that They who sought Gain by Lottery would Burn and the Worm Gnore their Vitals. Four tourists on the Australian run wrote to enquire how they could fix a visit to Kolumbe Reserve, and someone calling himself Pensioner sent three pages blistering me because the Quiz hadn't been properly advertised. He should, he said, most certainly have won it.

I hung around the flat all day in case the 'phone rang. At four-thirty I was down at the *Chronicle* again for the second sorting of mail. This brought me a square envelope with a single sheet of paper in it. The message was brief.

Percy Kennedy is Mynah (P.K.) he's not here if you want to know where to send his money you can ring 363-3152 Tuesday evening six o'clock and ask for Lola.

I went home and checked with the telephone exchange. 363-3152 was the number of the Gloriana Café in Point Road. That's down near the docks. I'd have liked to arrange for someone to watch the café while I 'phoned, but there wasn't time. I filled in what I did have, studying the note.

There was something greedy about the phrasing, I thought, and the writing was greedy too. Possibly it was just a chancer trying to grab one hundred rand, but maybe not.

So sharp at six I rang the number.

It didn't sound a classy place. There was a juke-box playing and someone yelling over it in what sounded like Greek. I asked for Lola. In a few moments a tired, gritty voice said, "Lola speaking". I said I was the Secretary for the Kolumbe Quiz Competition and was 'phoning in answer to an application for one of the prizes by or on behalf of a Mr Percy Kennedy.

"Yeah. That's right. He's Mynah. You can send me the cash. This address is safe."

"I'm afraid there are certain formalities to be completed first. May I have your name?"

A pause. "Lola Kennedy."

"Mrs?"

"Miss."

"Miss Kennedy, unfortunately I'm only allowed to hand over the prize money to the candidate himself."

"I told you, he's not here, he's in Rhodesia."

"You're in touch with him? Maybe a relation?"

A sigh. "His sister."

"Can you produce proof of identity, and of your relationship to Mr Kennedy?"

"Look," the voice was impatient. "Percy won the prize, didn't he, 'at's his nom-de-plume, Mynah. Well then?"

"I can't hand over any money until I'm authorised to do so by the winner."

"I'm acting on Percy's instructions."

"I can't take your word for that." I waited. Each of us was bluffing. I knew she was, she probably knew I was. I wondered what she looked like. Her voice interested me.

It was phoney; not trying to be cultured, but the other way about, an educated voice that's been adapted to please tougher company. She might be Point Road now, but she could have been Michael Crescent before The Fall.

I said, "Look, Miss Kennedy, if you can obtain written authority from your brother, and post it to me, I'll ask my committee to consider it. Thank you for getting in touch with me. Goodbye."

"Wait!" I could hear her breathing into the receiver as if she'd shifted it under her chin and was using her hands to write, or signal someone to her side. "Maybe we could meet? Talk about it?"

"There's not much to discuss, is there?"

"My brother will be down from Rhodesia soon." The voice had lost some of its huskiness and become decisive. "Do you know the Hurly Burly?"

"Yes."

"I could meet you there. Say Thursday morning? Eight

o'clock. I work shifts, so that'd suit. I'm stout and not tall. I'll carry an orange patent leather handbag."

"Very well. Eight, at the Hurly Burly."

"Hy, I don't know your name."

I ignored that. "I'll be wearing a cream slack-suit with a gold spider buckle on the belt. I have red hair and a long nose, you can't miss me." I put the receiver firmly back on its rest.

No sooner had I done so than the doorbell rang. I went across and found the caretaker on the step. He held out an envelope.

"Delivered by hand, Miss Bryant. An African chauffeur. I thought, better bring it straight up than leave it lie in the box."

"Thanks, Mr Shulze."

The letter was from Mrs Dessels. Elegant, precise writing in black ink on thick cream paper. I was invited, with or without companion, to take morning coffee on Wednesday at 11.00 a.m. It would be a pleasure to meet a Bryant again, after all these years.

I telephoned Dave Leatherhead, who was out, but I left a message that I'd pick him up at 10.00 a.m. tomorrow.

Finally I 'phoned Evan and asked him to go with me to the Hurly Burly at eight o'clock on Thursday morning to meet a Miss Lola Kennedy, sister of Percy Kennedy, alias Mynah, P.K.

Evan started firing questions at me, but I told him my bath-water was overflowing and hung up.

One way and another I felt pretty smug about my day's work.

It just goes to show the truth of the old adage, that fat head often wins thick ear.

⑤ ⑤ ⑤

XVI

NEITHER DAVE NOR I found time to admire the coastal scenery on the way out, because we were too busy quarrelling. It started when Dave asked if I'd seen the advert in the paper and I said yes, and he said whoever put it in was a psychopathic nut. I didn't say anything and he asked if I'd put it in and I said thanks for the compliment. After that every subject seemed to go sour on us. We got on to politics and the W.C.C. vote on money for terrorists, and in no time at all we were shouting. One of the boring things about being a left-wing South African is that everyone hammers you. The reactionaries at home call you a Communist and a Sickly Liberalist. The instant demos abroad accuse you of expediency. The silly thing was that though Dave and I were on the same side, we still yelled at each other. By the time we reached La Gratitude it was deep freeze. We drove from the village to the beach in silence and he refused to come into the house with me.

It was the sort of beach cottage I'd expected, old, built of cement blocks and corrugated iron with a lot of wind-bitten pines at the back and a clump of skinny geraniums round the door. But the glorious old sea was singing sagas not a hundred yards away, and the air had the sharp silvery glint of salt.

I knocked on the back door and got ready to face the muzzle-loaders, but an African cook told me kindly that Madam was on the beach with the grandchildren and would I please come in and sit down and wait.

The ten minutes wait saved me from making a bigger fool of myself than usual. The living-room was an enormous square with pine floorboards, dead-beat rugs and faded covers, but the Africana in it must have been worth many thousand rands. The whole of one wall was books, some of them folios of original cartoons that I'd have given a lot to examine. There were at least three pictures that belonged in a National Gallery, and a magnificent woodcut by Khumalo, flanked on one side by a child's cross-stitch map of La Gratitude, and on the other by a calendar advertising Gordon's Gin. On the centre table was a Sithole woodcarving and a Radebe bronze. I was still gaping at the bronze when Mrs Dessels came in.

"Miss Bryant, I am so sorry to keep you waiting. My daughter's children are with me and we spend our days on the beach."

"Please don't apologise. It's given me a chance to enjoy your lovely things."

"Yes, I keep them all round me. The sea air is bad for them but I don't care." She came and took my hand. "I see you like the Radebe."

"It's wonderful. I haven't seen much of his work."

"He gave it to me before he went into exile. Would you like tea or coffee? Or a cold drink?"

Coffee was brought in a blue-and-white Delft service that looked old enough to make me nervous. While my hostess was dealing with the tray I got a good look at her. Evan's talk about Boer Generals had made me expect someone fit only for the archives. Mrs Dessels didn't look much above sixty-five. She had the sort of face I associate with the Highveld. Neat-featured, with slanting cheekbones and milky-blue, rather humourless eyes. Her hair was hardly touched with grey and the thick mass of it was plaited round her head, with bangs on the forehead that looked very mod, somehow. Her hands were large and competent with big oval nails. She wore a blue cotton beach dress; and sandals on feet that glistened with grains of dry sand.

"So, Miss Bryant, you follow in your aunt's footsteps? You are working the Kolumbe clays again, I hear."

"Yes."

"She was a fine artist, and a very beautiful woman." The milky eyes regarded me thoughtfully. "She would ride past our house with a hawk on her wrist. She enjoyed the hunt."

"So I'm told."

"And now you want to talk to me. About her, not so?"

"You're very clever to guess that."

"No. Not clever. Logical. You read the article in the *Chronicle*, like the rest of us. It has disturbed you. Did you see the advertisement also?"

"Yes."

"And what did you make of it?"

"Very little."

"That is because you're too young to remember." She paused. "Although I remember you, as a very young child, when your father brought you to Kolumbe. Did you send that story to the *Chronicle*, Miss Bryant?"

"No, Mrs Dessels. I don't know who did."

"Nor does the Editor. I enquired." A perfectly steady hand offered me a cup of coffee. "Of course it was someone who wished to harm my son Johan."

"How can you be sure?"

"I am sure. He was the only one who loved Kate and therefore the only one who could be hurt."

"What about my father? He loved her. So did Gretha Corbitt."

"One is dead, the other mentally deranged, so both are beyond hurt. No, it is clear the thing was aimed at Johan. I thought you might be responsible, that is why I allowed you to come here today."

She gave me a hesitant smile that took the sting out of the words. "I think, now I've met you, that you aren't that sort of person? To harbour a grudge? You're more like Kate, I think, more likely to come quickly to blows and forget the cause as quickly. It's very strange, you know, to see you sitting there. I thought I had seen the last of your family. Well, since it is otherwise decreed, our only hope lies in frankness. How much do you know about Johan and Kate?"

"I'm told they were lovers."

"No. It might have been better if they had been. It is very difficult to explain. You don't know my son."

She folded her hands together and bent her head over them for a moment, then looked straight at me. "People accuse me of being possessive. Perhaps I am, but the relationship between mother and child is too complicated and delicate to be

84

described in a sentence. My own marriage was unhappy. As soon as the older boys were grown, my husband and I sold the farm at Kolumbe, and separated. He moved to Muden, I came here. Johan came with me. He resembled me in nature, so we were very close.

"He was a brilliant student both at school and at university, so brilliant that he graduated far too young. He was always shy and inept with other people his own age. He has never been capable of spontaneous emotion, he is obtuse about what lies in the hearts and minds of other human beings. He is idealistic and strait-laced. In all this he resembles me. I neither excuse nor acclaim. That is how we are.

"And this son of mine loved Kate Falconer. Can you imagine anything more unsuitable, more likely to cause him unhappiness?

"He loved her from the time he was a boy. A child. At Kolumbe, he would go over always to the Falconers' house. When the family moved back to town, Johan was miserable. From this childish adoration came the total commitment of the man. Johan was a scientist who cared nothing for the arts; an Afrikaner; a puritan who disliked excess in any form; a conventional creature who thought of women in terms of marriage and the home. He disliked and despised almost every factor in Kate's environment, at times he disliked and despised her own actions and life, and yet for Kate the person he felt the most intense devotion.

"He was bitterly jealous of her. He hated every man who looked at her, and there were very many of these. I can tell you stories . . . Nick Corbitt, for instance. People believed the resentment between Nick and Johan was because of the war. Nick was a hero and Johan never even joined the Army. It was nothing to do with the war. Johan was far more use as a back-room boy. He did good work there, and never felt he'd been cheated of a chance to serve. The reason he quarrelled with Nick was because Kate liked him. Nick was witty and gallant, he flirted with Kate and made her laugh. He could reach a frivolous streak in her that was quite beyond Johan. You see, Kate found life a little ridiculous. She liked to tease and be teased. She laughed at herself and at others. Johan can't bear to be mocked.

"At first, I blamed Kate for encouraging him. She took him on trips with her. I thought, used him. Then as I watched her work develop, I saw that what she got from him was something she truly needed. His knowledge of animals is expressed in many of her early models, before her line became more abstract. And she gave him an ability to break out of his own confining limits. With her, he was more like other men. It was not a physical liaison, but they were linked by the intellect, by common interests. It was a sort of love between them, but of course it could not be total, nor permanent. I tried to make Johan understand that.

"He thought I was interfering out of jealousy. Oh, it is so painful to stand by and watch while your son destroys himself! Finally I realised I could say nothing. I must just wait. I did wait, I was patient, I held my tongue.

"And when Kate decided to go to London for the exhibition, I hoped the break might come. She left. Johan seemed busy, and reasonably happy. I began to hope it was over. Then Deirdre. . . your mother . . . fell ill. I remember Johan came home and told me it was encephalitis. He was very quiet. After a little while he said to me, 'Kate will come home,' and I looked at him and his face was shining.

"So the thing was not finished. Kate returned, too late to see your mother. In her grief, she became wild and restless. You will have been told. Still Johan persisted in seeing her. He would hang about on the fringe of the parties, waiting for a few minutes with Kate. He told me, 'One day she will turn to me.' He believed it. It was pathetic to see how he deluded himself.

"Then Kate found someone else." Mrs Dessels turned her face towards me but her eyes were blank. She remained quite still for a while and then gave a tiny shake of the head, and said almost under her breath, "That is the only explanation. She found someone else. It was what I had always been afraid of."

I said, "Did you know the man?" Mrs Dessels' eyes focused on me again.

"I? No. It didn't matter who, he existed. One could see, Kate was like a hill-fire. And my poor Johan was going out of his mind. I can't describe to you what those last weeks were like. He was obsessed. Never still. He would be away for days at a time. I think he stayed in town, trying to talk to Kate. He was thirty years old and a man of repute but he behaved like a green boy. He bought her presents, importuned her friends, he crawled. It was a humiliation to watch him. I begged him to save at least some dignity. We all knew Kate was lost to him. Useless. He wouldn't listen. He was deaf, blind, mad.

"I went to see Kate Falconer, myself." Mrs Dessels' clenched hand beat softly on the arm of her chair. "I asked her to end it quickly, for Johan and for me. She told me she had tried. That was the first time I realised that Kate was both a good and a kind woman.

"Yes, good and kind. We talked a long time. At the end she said, 'Don't worry, Mrs Dessels. It won't be long now. A few weeks more.' She told me that she had planned a special occasion for October 31st. Hallowe'en. She said, 'I've invited Johan. Let him come. I give you my promise it will be my farewell party and after that I won't be here to cause any more trouble.' And she smiled and gave me a kiss.

"She was happy when she said that. Afterwards, I thought about it often, and I'm sure she was happy. She was not speaking of death.

"Our meeting consoled me. It's so much easier to be stoical when there is a limit set. I thought, after Hallowe'en it will be finished; and I was easier in my mind. In fact I did not have to wait so long. Kate told Johan on October 30th that she would not see him again.

"It was a terrible night, but I thought at the time it was blessed for us. Johan had gone in to Durban, to see Kate. There was a crowd of people at her house, chattering and drinking. He couldn't get her alone. He waited and waited, and at last she came out on to the terrace where he was standing and spoke to him. He asked her again to marry him. She refused. She said it was over and done with and he must not try to see her again. She would not stay to discuss it, she said she had to go out almost at once. She said goodnight and kissed him on the cheek and walked off along the terrace. He never saw her again.

"He came back here in a terrible state. He knew it was final. Half of him couldn't accept, the other half knew it was final. There was only one thing I could do to help him, and that was

87

leave him alone. In a few hours, he made up his mind. He packed his things and went away, right out of the country. He was away for seven months. I don't even know how he learned about Kate's death. I wrote to him but he never answered the letter. He just put her out of his life for good."

Mrs Dessels fell silent. Her cloudy gaze wandered, as if she had forgotten I was there.

I said, "It could have happened differently."

"What?" The eyes were alert enough now.

"Mrs Dessels, a man like your son, crazy in love and jealous as they come, wouldn't say goodbye to Kate and leave it that way. She tells him she's finished with him. Perhaps tells him there's someone else. She says she can't stop because she has another engagement, and she walks out of his life. And you think Johan just let her go?"

"I've told you . . ."

"Yes, and I don't believe it. You know, there was a story in the newspapers that Kate was seen crossing the border, in a man's company, a few days after she went missing. The Swaziland border, I think it was. Where did Johan go?"

She made no answer, just glared at me.

"I agree, I don't think Kate went to Swaziland, with or without your son. The police must have checked. I think what happened is Kate went to Kolumbe, and Johan followed her there."

"No." Her face was very pale. "That is not true, Miss Bryant."

"Sure again, I see."

"I trust Johan. Whatever his faults, he doesn't tell lies."

"Oh, my God, he's a grown man, not a little boy. Every man tells lies in certain circumstances. I wouldn't blame anyone who tried to keep clear of scandal. No one wants to read their own love-life in the Sunday press, so if Johan went to Kolumbe, he'd shut up about it. That's all."

"You are graceless and impertinent."

"Yeah, I know I am, but at least I'm not trying to bury Kate Falconer before she's dead. You have some fine *objets d'art* round here, Mrs Dessels, but nothing of hers. That's interesting, to me."

Her mouth moved spasmodically. "Johan doesn't wish it."

"Out of sight, out of mind. Epitaph for an artist."

"Go away." She was leaning back in her chair, her eyes closed. She looked shaken out of her wits and I felt ashamed. I went over to her and took one of her wrists. The pulse was perfectly steady. The eyes flew open and glared at me. She was neither sick nor scared, just furious.

"Mrs Dessels, I want to talk to your son."

"To check my story, I suppose?"

"No. I'm going to see everyone who was invited to Kate's farewell party."

"How do you know . . . ?" she began, and then folded her mouth.

"Gretha Corbitt gave me the list," I said. I let her wrist fall and straightened up. "I'm sorry I was rude to you. But you said frankness was our only hope."

She leaned there looking up at me, and her face slowly fell back into its serene lines. You could see her gathering up the skirts of rage and shaking them smooth. She even managed a gracious smile. "I rest before lunch," she said. "I'm growing rather old and tired. I assure you, Miss Bryant, if Johan were here he would tell you precisely what I have told you. But so far as I know he is in East Africa, and unlikely to return for many months."

"I see." I didn't envy her her collection any more, she seemed too darned lonely. I said, "Mrs Dessels, thank you for talking to me, you've helped me a lot. Goodbye."

For a moment she really looked at me. She said in a low voice, "Girl, let the past alone. It's a hearth of dead ashes." Then she closed her eyes, and I went out of the house into the sun.

The Volvo had been moved to the lee of the pine-trees. Dave Leatherhead was drowsing in the passenger seat. He sat up abruptly as I approached.

"Lennie, I apologise."

"Hmh?" I couldn't think what he was talking about until I remembered the argument on the way up. "Oh, don't be silly." I climbed into the car and started the engine.

"You look greenish," he said.

"I was rude and graceless."

"More so than usual?"

"Is that really how I seem?"

He grinned. "No. Why did you lose your rag?"

"She spun me a tale. She deliberately invited me out here to spin me a tale about her son and I nearly believed it."

"What made you change your mind?"

"Don't know." A doubt hit me. "It could be that all she said was true. Maybe I'm just obsessed. But there was none of Kate's work in that room. Khumalo, Radebe, all the other local boys are represented, but not Kate. Mrs Dessels lived for years at Kolumbe, she should have a piece."

"Perhaps Johan doesn't want it around."

"I'd say Mrs Dessels doesn't want it around. She still feels that way, twenty years after Kate's death. Yet she told me that Kate was a good, kind woman, and I think she meant it. A funny mixture. She's clever, too. She told me nine-tenths of the truth, but I'm sure the last tenth is what matters."

Dave didn't answer directly. He said, "Did you ask her where Johan is now?"

"She told me, East Africa."

"Then your doubts are well placed." He held out his hand. On the palm lay an oblong luggage label. I slowed down to look at it.

DR JOHAN DESSELS

"There's an old Ford truck with a canopy in one of the Dessels' sheds," Dave told me. "Padlock on the door but the screws were rotten. I took a decco. The truck has East Africa plates and it's covered with dirt. A lot of clobber in the back, equipment and specimens, all tagged with the same label. I'll make you a small bet, my lovely, that while you were in the cottage talking to Mama, son Johan was on the other side of the door, listening to every word."

XVII

B ECAUSE IT WAS past noon, we went to Kolumbe for lunch. After we'd eaten, Dave fell asleep in a deck-chair on the lawn, and I went and collected Freya from the barn and took her out hunting. I took her right up the hill behind the house before I removed her hood. She spent about twenty minutes lazing about the sky and then killed a wood pigeon. I left her to devour it and went and sat on a rock and looked down at the home acres.

I could see Dave lying like a doll in his chair, and far away on my left the double curve of the river with the blue kidney of Kolumbe island in midstream. That's where Kate's dinghy was found. Only a very strong swimmer could cross the estuary at floodtide. I wondered how many of her friends had known that, and how they must have felt, waiting for news while the beaters combed the banks for her body.

How did Johan Dessels feel? Whatever he'd suffered, he'd shared it with no one. Had he really been at his mother's cottage this morning? Had he come home because of the article in the newspaper? If so, it carried a pretty powerful message. I wondered if my advertisement had brought any more answers. Tomorrow, I'd go and see.

The sun beat on my back and the wind was soft and warm. I dozed, my brain full of gold sparks of thought that seemed to die before I could catch hold of them.

At half-past three I whistled Freya back and walked slowly down to the barn. Old Jacob, the *induna* of the labour team, was working on a tractor in the repair yard and I talked to him for a while. He asked me who was the young man with the camera. I told him, a friend from overseas, and Jacob laughed and said he must be very rich if he could afford to pay an *umfaan* by the stream one rand for a clay buffalo.

When I reached the house, Dave was back in his chair, examining his loot.

"I hear some Infant Moses conned you out of a rand for that?"

"No conning about it. I could get three times what I paid, in London. Genuine primitive is very popular. But I shall keep it. Souvenir de Kolumbe. What does the name mean?"

"It's a distortion from Colombe. The Mauritian immigrants found doves in the bush. The Zulus took over the name and the English spelled it as if it were Zulu."

"That's very nice." Dave stroked the buffalo. "Is this the clay you use?"

"No, that's coarse white. There's a finer one we use for firing purposes, and we have good black and red."

"Would you give me one of your own things, some day?"

I hesitated. I don't like handing over my work unless I'm sure about the person I give it to. Then I remembered how he'd promised me his photographs, and felt ashamed. "Of course I will."

It was after four o'clock when we started back for Durban. Dave said very little on the way in. I'd told him all about my interview with Mrs Dessels, and perhaps, like me, he was going over that in his mind.

I dropped him at his hotel and thought about calling on Evan at once, but decided against it. I went back to the flat and parked the Volvo and collected my mail from the front foyer, and then I took the lift up and walked straight across the corridor and put my key in the lock.

The man must have been hiding on the stairway. I just felt one of his hands close on my neck and his other hand reached round me and turned the key, and the next moment I was being lifted through my own front door like a badly-tied parcel.

⌬ ⌬ ⌬

XVIII

THE MAN LET go of my neck once we were in the hallway, but he kept shoving me until we reached the living-room and then gave me a final jerk that spun me half across the floor. A voice like polar ice said, "Next time you come frightening my mother, Miss Bryant, I'll break you in half."

I caught my balance and backed off fast. He was standing between me and the telephone and I knew I'd no chance of reaching it. There was a gun in the flat, somewhere, unloaded. A blunt carving-knife in the kitchen. I got my fingers round the neck of the bottle of Tassheimer on the dresser, and tried to breathe evenly.

He didn't come any closer, just stood glaring at me. I saw that although he was big, he wasn't fit. His face was sallow under the tan and he was sweating too much. Something . . . or someone . . . had scarred one cheek for him, three white gouges that puckered the skin and made one eye seem a bit larger than the other. They were pale blue, like his mother's, and looked quite crazy. He wore white, top to toe, very cool and clinical. The mad doctor. I opened my mouth for a good loud scream and he shook his head in a bewildered sort of way and said, "Please don't. I'm sorry. I didn't mean to hurt you."

For a man who planned to break me in half, it was a handsome apology. I took a firmer grip on the bottle and said, "You get the hell out of my flat."

"No, please." He raised a hand. "I lost my temper. Lost my head. I'm not well, you see, and my mother was so upset it upset me. Please, cannot we talk?"

He was trembling now like an exhausted horse. He moved across the room and dropped into the armchair by the window. He said, "Perhaps you would give me a little of that wine?"

So the next thing was, I was pouring Tassheimer into my best Swedish crystal. I handed him the glass and then took up a position facing him, but with the door right behind me.

"Dr Dessels . . ." I began, and again he held up the hand.

"One moment. I must explain. I had an argument with my mother. She had no right to discuss me with you. When she told me what she had said, I was angry. I have been ill with malaria and find it hard to sustain the proper calm. I drove into town, thinking I would see you. You were not here. I waited on the stairs for four hours. It was foolish but that is what I did. Waited. And then you came, walking as she used to, carefree. It seemed a mockery. Not by you. A mockery by the years, of everything I have endured. You don't understand, how should you?" He set the glass carefully on the floor beside him and looked at me. "I want to finish it. I don't care how, it's time it was over."

"Kate is dead, Dr Dessels. You know that."

He sat quietly looking at me. It was odd, as his temper faded, how his whole appearance changed. He was just a big, sick man with sweat on his forehead and a puzzled expression in his eyes. He fumbled a cigar-case from his pocket and lit one. I put an ashtray beside him and he thanked me politely.

"Dead, yes, but not forgotten. One should be allowed to forget. Miss Bryant, why did you write to my mother?"

I thought about that and decided to speak the truth. "Because I wanted to trace you. Because you were one of the twelve people due to attend Kate's farewell party."

"But why do you mention that? It never took place."

"I know. If I knew why, I'd know who killed her."

"Killed?" His eyes were as cold as a squid's. "Killed?"

"Your mother lied to me, Doctor. She told me a pretty story about how you said goodnight to Kate at my father's house, and she walked away along the terrace, and you never saw her again. I don't believe it. You saw her again, at Kolumbe."

"That is a slanderous statement."

"But you won't bring any case; because the night of October 30th 1946, is something you don't even like to remember, let alone talk about in court. You certainly never mentioned it at the inquest."

"I was not at the inquest. I was out of the country."

"Having left the day after Kate disappeared? Very convenient. You followed her to Kolumbe that night, didn't you?"

"What are you suggesting?"

"Let me take a guess. You tried to speak to her in Michael Crescent, but the place was crowded with guests. When you did talk to her, she told you she was going away and wouldn't see you again. You watched her movements, saw her go into the house and come out a little later with her overnight bag. When she drove off in her car, you followed her, to the shack at Kolumbe. That's where she always went when she was worried, or needed time to think.

"At the shack, you were alone with her. No witnesses. What did she say to you, Dr Dessels? Did she tell you the reason she was leaving town, that there was another man? Did you lose your temper with her, the way you did with me, grab her by the throat? Did you hit her, strangle her, break her in half?"

He started to claw himself out of the chair and I jumped for the door, but then I saw that his face showed nothing but a total, horrified denial. He cried out, "Wait! Oh my good girl, wait, whatever is all this you're saying?"

"Someone killed Kate." My voice seemed to be going up and down and I couldn't steady it. "Someone killed her and you were the last person to talk to her and you had reason to kill her. I know how you behaved, the last few months of her life. Your own mother admits you were obsessed."

He sank back in the chair. His mouth pulled back in a grimace and he waved a hand with a sort of weary impatience.

"Sit down. Sit down and listen."

I sat, but near the door.

"I did follow Kate to Kolumbe," he said. "She knew I was doing so, we agreed upon it. It was impossible to talk at Ralph's, all those parakeets squawking. Kate was tired. She had had arguments with Ralph and others. There were money difficulties and she thought things were being wrongly handled, but these were trivial matters. I was not interested in them. I told her so. I told her she must give me time to talk, she owed me that much. She said, 'I'm going to the farm. You can come there, if you like.' And that was what happened.

95

"We drove to the shack. We sat on the verandah and drank coffee. We talked. I asked her to marry me, as I had done many times before, and as usual she refused. She told me she was leaving Durban and would prefer not to see me again for a time. She told me she would always value me and need me, but as a friend. It was most conventional and correct, you see?"

He looked at the stub of the cigar he held, and almost abstractly flicked it out of the window. "I don't know where you got this extraordinary picture of violence. I assure you I did not shout or plead, or lose my temper. Oh, I admit I had behaved badly before. I behaved badly after, but on that night I was perfectly calm. And my dear child . . ." he smiled at me with sad eyes . . . "I loved Kate far too much to harm her in any way."

"If that's how it was, conventional and correct, why didn't you ever tell the police, or my father, you were at Kolumbe with Kate? You suppressed evidence."

"I know I did. By the time the police questioned me it was six weeks later, in Mozambique. The thing was already a major scandal. What could I do, go back to Durban, provide more meat for the vultures, give them my life to strip to the bone? It wouldn't bring Kate back. She was drowned, gone. I said nothing. At the time it seemed the right thing. I've regretted it since."

I believed him. I don't know why, but I did. I said, "Did Kate tell you anything else?"

"She said there was a man. She would marry him if she married at all. She spoke of a child."

"You mean she was pregnant."

"I don't know," said Dessels simply. "I didn't ask her. After she refused me, I didn't stay long. I wanted to be by myself."

"Did she say who the man was?"

"No."

"You couldn't guess?"

"Of what use are guesses? Naturally, I wondered. Nick Corbitt? A man called Greco? She saw them both frequently. What does this matter now?"

"Could she have loved a man like Greco?"

"A fox is beautiful and clever despite its stink. Kate liked cleverness."

96

"Did he want her?"

"Oh yes. He collected women. I warned her to be careful of him. He was a bad man."

"You weren't afraid of him?"

"Why should I be?"

"As a rival."

"Unsuccessful. Greco knew that."

"Was Kate afraid of him?"

"She didn't fear anyone, that was the trouble. But Greco? I think she found him amusing, nothing more. He was no threat to her."

"If she turned him down?"

"He'd laugh it off."

"I'm told Greco never forgave an injury."

"From a woman? I doubt if any woman could injure him. It would be beneath his dignity. Greco's only real interest was money. If Kate did him out of that, then, perhaps . . ."

"Let's say she did double-cross him in some way. Would he be capable of killing her, and faking the drowning incident?"

"This is quite ridiculous . . . I've told you . . ."

"Would he?"

"Greco might organise violence, but he'd certainly never risk his own neck. He was the sort to hire his hangmen."

"A Jacky Hangman?"

"What?"

"A shrike? Like Cory Bergen?"

Johan Dessels stared at me. "Perhaps."

"Cory would kill for money?"

"Big money, maybe." Dessels shivered. "This is a nightmare. Why do you say these things? They're not bearable. I'm ill, you know, I can't listen to all this."

I moved towards his chair. "Gretha Corbitt spoke to me a short while ago. She told me Kate was not dead, but sleeping. The way she spoke, made me think someone had drummed the phrase into her."

Dessels frowned. "To comfort a child one says such words."

"Or to convince a grown woman who's a bit simple that she hasn't seen a dead body?"

97

Now he did get to his feet, slowly, and stood swaying a little, watching me.

I said, "Gretha was always unbalanced, but after Kate disappeared she was stone crazy. Something happened. Something terrible happened to Kate and Gretha knew about it. She shares the knowledge with at least one other person, Cory Bergen. That's why she's so scared of him."

Dessels shook his head. "You're out of your mind."

"No I'm not, and nor is Gretha. Not on all points, at any rate."

"All nonsense," he muttered, but he kept his eyes on me. Suddenly he said in quite a different voice, "Who told you about the party?"

"Evan Cruickshank."

"And the list of people invited? I never knew there were twelve. How did you find out?"

"Gretha told me."

"That's very strange."

"It was a strange party. Twelve guests, making thirteen at the table, with Kate. And why did she leave out old friends like Evan, yet invite a man like Jean-Charles Greco?"

"Chance," said Dessels. "Caprice." But he didn't sound as if he believed it.

I went to the desk and took out the box of Hallowe'en trinkets. I brought it over to Dessels and took out the one with the ostrich on it, and gave it to him.

"What's this?" He seemed genuinely puzzled.

"A party favour, made for you by Kate."

He thrust it back at me as if it burned his skin. I chose another charm. "Look at the workmanship, Doctor. Each design is different, each piece is fired and glazed. Kate must have planned her party well in advance."

He studied the favour on my palm, and a sudden stillness touched his face. It was as if something in him, detached and enquiring, pushed emotion aside. He put out a finger and traced the figure on the china. It was the pelican, with the initials M.S.

I said softly, "Who does it represent?"

To my amazement, Dessels chuckled. "Morty Silke."

98

"You know him?"

But I'd spoken too fast. Dessels' head lifted sharply. He dropped the favour back in the box.

"I know nothing of the people Kate invited. I never meant to go to the party. I saw her for the last time at Kolumbe on October 30th and at eleven o'clock the next night I left for Swaziland, alone, as the police and border posts confirmed. I did not return to South Africa for seven months."

He was putting on another identity, Johan Dessels, Doctor of Science, recluse. He said, "I have made my life. I do not wish to discuss the past. I do not wish to remember it. I wish to be left in peace."

He walked towards the door, turned and gave me a stiff little bow. "Goodbye, Miss Bryant. Thank you for the wine."

I didn't try to stop him. Talking to him had made me feel sad, and humble. He might be cold and unapproachable, as Evan said. You couldn't call him sociable, or charming. But I could see why Kate liked him. He was a real person, who suffered and made mistakes and didn't forget the people he loved.

I put the favours back in the desk, and picked up the telephone book to see if the name Silke was listed. It wasn't. I tried Silk and Sylke and even Mortimer-Silke, but there was nothing. I was sitting turning the pages in a dispirited sort of way when there came a knock on the door. I thought it might be Dessels back again, and took a cautious look through the seeing-eye device in the door; but it was Evan Cruikshank who stood in the corridor. He started to rattle the door handle and yell, "Lennie, open up."

I did so. Evan was scarlet and breathless and his hair stood up in tufts.

"There's been an accident. Over at Gretha Corbitt's. Half the place has collapsed and she's underneath."

I grabbed my coat and purse and followed Evan to the lift. In the downstairs foyer Evan said, "There's police and the fire brigade and God knows who over there."

"Will we get through?"

Evan hesitated. "Maybe not. Can you 'phone?"

So I stopped at the public telephone in the foyer and called the Sharveys' number. I expected a servant to answer, or perhaps Cory Bergen, but it was Nell who spoke. It put me off my stroke and I stammered, "Mrs Sharvey? I mean Nell? It's Lennie Bryant. I've just heard . . ."

She interrupted me. "Thank God. I wanted to 'phone you but there are so many people, and I couldn't . . ." Her voice dropped as if she were speaking very close to the receiver. "Lennie, we must talk. Can you come down here?"

"Of course. But Gretha? Is there any chance?"

"They're digging. Come at once. I'll tell the policeman on the gate to let you through. Hurry."

⑤ ⑤ ⑤

XIX

EVAN DROVE ME down to Michael Crescent. He parked his car in Peak Road and walked round with me. There was already a crowd in the lamplight at the end of the cul-de-sac. They looked like spectres on Walpurgis Night.

I told the policeman on the gate who I was and he waved us on, but Evan said he wouldn't go in, so I went up the drive alone. About a dozen vehicles were parked on the turn-around at the front-door, including a couple of patrol cars and a fire engine. Someone had rigged up two powerful arc-lights on a truck and these shone on the façade of the house.

At first I couldn't think what looked so wrong with that, and then I realised the huge old hedge was down. Part of the front wall of Gretha's flat had come down with it. I could see the entrails of the house, a sliding, crazy tangle of wood and brick and junk that seemed ready to come crashing into the garden any moment.

Over the whole wreck, men worked with ladders and ropes. I saw Derek Sharvey among them, but no sign of Nick or Cory Bergen. There were fire ladders up to the windows of Gretha's living-room, and a coloured welder was working on the bars with a blow-torch. As I stood watching, a fireman passed and I grabbed his arm.

"Have they found her?"

"Lady, they haven't found no one. There's tons of stuff in there. We can't use the doors. If we shift from the bottom the whole blerry lot comes down, so we must go in by the top and lift it off. You a friend of the lady lived there?"

"My father knew her, a long time ago."

He squinted at me, rubbing a grimy hand down his stubble. "Why'd they let her live that way? Keeping all that junk, man, it's crazy."

"She was mentally ill."

"So why di'n't they shut her up safe? If she's lucky, she's a'ready dead. I told the other lady ... her sister, is it? ... to keep away. She won't want to see what we'll find, dead or alive." He turned away and went back to his task.

I crossed the driveway and found the French doors to Nick's room standing open. A faint glimmer of light showed. A voice called, "Lennie? Come in."

Nell Sharvey was waiting for me, a half-shadow in the arm-chair behind the desk. A single lamp burned at her side, and from the walls glinted the glass of Nick's regimental groups, the metal of his guns and trophies.

As I walked towards her, Nell dropped the receiver of a telephone back on the rest.

"I'm still trying to reach Nick. He and Cory went up to Pinetown to the wrought-iron factory." She slowly opened a cigarette box on the desk, took one, pushed the box towards me. Her fingers turned the cigarette over and over. Her big hazel eyes watched me with an abstracted expression. "Do you realise," she said, "that if it had happened four days earlier, you might have been in there with her? That was my first thought, thank God no one else was in there with her."

Her mouth began to twitch and she pressed one hand against it, staring at me. I sat down in a chair near the lamp. "Can you tell me how it happened?"

"A noise," she said. "All these years, I've been expecting trouble, and when it came, I couldn't move, I just stood. I was upstairs. It began like thunder, and the whole house shook. It seemed to go on and on. Then I ran. Downstairs, out into the garden. The wall was down and the hedge. There was dust in a great cloud. When it settled, there wasn't a sound. I was afraid to call her. I waited there in the sun, and the servants came running."

"She may be alive. Nell, only part of the house was crammed, her own rooms were quite clear."

Nell pinched her lower lip between finger and thumb. She seemed to hear me with difficulty. At last she shook her head. "The firemen put ladders up to all the windows. They called. Gretha never made a sound, nor did Lorca. They're dead. She must have heard someone and gone down. The stuff shifted, somehow."

I knew I should tell her about the trip wires, but I couldn't make myself. She was too far in shock. I sat dumb and after a moment she said, "Did you speak to anyone?"

"A fireman."

"What did he say?"

"That there wasn't much chance."

She nodded slowly. Her eyes filled with tears. "People won't understand. They'll blame us. But we had no choice, short of having her certified. We couldn't do that."

"I suppose it might have saved her life."

"What sort of life do you live in an asylum? For Gretha, to leave here would be an end of living. It was better to let her make her own prison, like the rest of us."

Her anxious eyes scanned mine and the tears began to slide down her cheeks. She made no effort to wipe them away but instead picked up a box of matches and started to fumble with it. I got up and took it from her and lit her cigarette. The fingers she put out to touch mine were cold as snow. I went over to a side-table where I could see some decanters, and found the brandy and poured a shot into a glass. When I gave it to her, she took a couple of sips and then set the glass aside, but the liquor seemed to calm her, because when she spoke again her voice was steady.

"Lennie, there's no time for grief. I called you here because we must decide what we're going to say. The police and the press will ask questions." She blew out smoke and it coiled gently over the smooth planes of her hair. "Frankly, my wish is to protect my family from publicity. There will be scandal about Gretha. Let that be all. I don't want the old quarrels revived. Nick can't face that again. I will take the blame for allowing Gretha to live as she did. I can defend myself against the present, but I have little defence against the past. Pressmen are acute. They're quick to sense the connection between incidents. We mustn't allow them to draw conclusions that will damage us. Must we?"

"I'm not sure what you mean."

Her large hand rose and fell. "It's clear enough, surely? A fortnight ago the *Chronicle* published a story about Kate Falconer and the Crescent. Last weekend, you showed up here. This afternoon there was the accident to Gretha. The police and the press will certainly look for answers to specific, obvious questions; for example, why you decided, after a lapse of twenty years, to renew your acquaintance with my family."

"If anyone asks me that," I said, "I think I shall tell the truth. I came here because someone is trying to raise the ghost of my aunt Kate. I came to meet the people she knew best, to try and find out why she quarrelled with them, and why she disappeared without trace on October 30th 1946."

She frowned at me and the colour rushed into her face. She took the cigarette from her mouth and laid it carefully on an ashtray. "Lennie, I don't think you can have listened to what I said. Don't you see that Kate's name must never be mentioned? Do you want to figure in the yellow press? More important, don't you see that to mention Kate would be to satisfy this anonymous crank? The whole thing is a malicious attack on us all, and we have to stop it forthwith. It must be stifled, or we can expect weeks of the most hideous notoriety. I know we can't avoid an uproar about Gretha, but let us at least keep silent on the subject of Kate."

"Gretha didn't agree with you there. She wanted to talk about

Kate, and I think she was right. There's been enough hushing up of unpleasant secrets."

She leaned towards me. The lamplight caught her eyes, wide, accusing. "Lennie? I believe you sent that story to the *Chronicle*!"

"No. But I can guess who did."

"Well?"

"Gretha." I was scared, now, and excited, and sure of myself. I didn't care whether or not I upset her, I meant to show her she wasn't going to dictate my words and actions. I repeated, "Gretha sent it."

Nell didn't contradict me. Her brows snapped together, and she said quickly, "Why would she do that?"

"Because she was beginning to remember what happened to Kate. I don't know what triggered it off. Perhaps my coming back from Europe. Maybe she saw my picture in the paper, something like that. I look like Kate."

"What did she say to you?"

"Enough to raise questions in my mind that you can answer. Like, why did you keep Gretha at home when she'd have been a lot better off in a hospital, getting psychiatric care? Did you believe she killed my aunt?"

Nell's eyes blazed at me. "Are you out of your mind?"

"No. Sane enough to see that Gretha loved Kate better than she ever loved you or any other member of your little set. Myself, I don't think she'd harm a fly, but it's possible you know better. Do you think she killed Kate to prevent her going away? Or out of jealousy? Is that why you've kept her locked away from the world, even from the doctors she needed? Because a medical man would know just how much of her talk was illusion, and how much was plain fact?"

Nell Sharvey sprang to her feet and came round the desk so quickly that she was bending over me before I could rise.

"Lennie, Lennie, you mustn't say such things. It's not only ridiculous, it's terribly dangerous. My dear, you can be hurt. Don't you see that?"

"You got me here to make sure our answers tallied, Mrs

Sharvey. I'm just giving you some of mine. I think Gretha could tell how my aunt died."

"Be quiet." Her hand gripped my shoulders with amazing strength. Her voice was calm and silvery like water running over me. "Think what you are saying."

"I know what I'm saying. I'm saying that you felt Gretha was capable of murder. You shut her away. You put out the story that Kate ran off with a lover. You used one scandal to conceal a greater one, and you succeeded. You'd have been safe for ever if someone hadn't sent a story to the *Chronicle*, and the most likely person to send it was the one you yourself called a prisoner. Gretha. Gretha making a bid to get out from behind the bars. Well, she tried, and now she's dead. What's your answer to that, Mrs Sharvey?"

Her face was so close that I could see the pallor of the skin and the film of sweat on the forehead. I was aware of the grip of her hands, of her eyes and her voice commanding me, and I was aware too of the fear in her. It seemed an age before she let me go and straightened up, and when she did, I still couldn't look away, or stop the trembling in my own body. All I could do was sit there and try and close my mind to the force of her will.

At length she moved away, to the far end of the desk. She stood watching me, the fingers of one hand lightly sweeping the surface of the wood. "You're clever," she said. "Clever, and very foolish at the same time. It was clever of you to guess that I was afraid for my sister, and foolish of you to think I could ever suspect her of violence. You had only to talk to her for half an hour to understand that she is gentle. I have never known her to hurt a single living thing. But you're right in saying I had to keep her near me. She was incapable of guarding her tongue. She knew too much for her own safety. Out in the world, she was in danger. Here at home, she was safe."

She put up a hand and smoothed the hair back from her forehead with a slow movement. "You see, Kate's death frightened us all. None of us dared to say so, but we all knew it was a terrible thing that had happened. She . . . there were people in her life who were wicked. Violent people. I warned her, but she was very stubborn, and reckless. She liked danger, I believe, and dangerous people. After her death, my one thought was to protect Gretha, and Nick. It was natural enough, wasn't it? You see, Lennie, neither of them could look after themselves. There was only me. I knew if I could just . . . withdraw them . . . keep them safe in Michael Crescent, show that none of us would question Kate's disappearance or make any accusations, then the trouble would pass. We'd be left in peace. I tried to tell Ralph, but he wouldn't listen. He couldn't understand that people like . . ." She stopped.

"Greco?" I said.

"You know about him?"

"Something."

"Then forget him," she said. "Please, Lennie, for your own sake, forget you ever heard about him. I thought we'd rid ourselves of him and his friends, but I was wrong. Don't you see, one of them has come back, to start it all over again? I don't know why, but I do know our only hope is to keep silent about the past, about Kate, about anything Gretha may have said to you, about anything you may guess or I may remember. Do you understand?"

It was strange how luminous her eyes seemed, in the broken light from the lamp. Her mouth curved in an expression that was both gentle and uncertain. This is Nell Sharvey, my mind said, who cared about Kate and who cares about you. She is wise and loving, do what she asks.

But at the back of my brain was the thought that if I kept silent, then Gretha was dead for no purpose. The world would forget her quickly enough. An end to Gretha, and to Kate Falconer as well. That was what Nell asked of me.

I began to struggle to my feet. Nell's long white hand stretched out to help me. Somehow I knew that if I grasped it, I'd never be free again, and I wanted to be free, I had to get out of that room and into the fresh air where I could breathe. I thrust her hand aside, stood up and shoved past her, making for the door.

"Lennie! Wait! You'll do as I say?"

I turned to answer her, but before I could do so, the front door slammed open, and voices erupted in the hall, loud and abrupt, arguing. There followed a brief pause during which I heard the thump of lumber falling on the lawn outside; and then rapid steps beat along the hall and Derek Sharvey appeared in the doorway.

"Nell. You're wanted."

Nell turned to face him. "They've found Gretha?"

"No. Nothing yet. But Nick's back and he's creating hell. He wants to go into the garden-flat, and the police have told him to keep away. They want you to restrain his ardour."

"Where's Cory?"

"Not back yet. Seems Nick and he didn't stay together in Pinetown. Nick gave him some commission or other."

Nell walked quickly out through the French windows. I started after her, but Sharvey stopped me with a gesture. "Leave them a moment. He's hysterical."

He stretched out a hand and pressed a wall-switch, flooding the study with light. Looking at him I was startled to see his little black eyes were blank and bright with shock. He went over to the drinks cabinet and poured himself a shot of whisky, drank it off and refilled the glass with plain soda. Over his shoulder he said, "Something for you?"

"No thank you."

He moved to the windows and stood frowning out, taking occasional swallows from the tumbler. "My advice to you, Miss Bryant, is get out before the questions start."

"I can't do that. I'm committed."

"More fool you." He swung round to face me. "You don't know the whole of it. There was a window open at the back of the house, forced open. And the front door was unlocked. Not on the chain. Gretha wouldn't leave it that way. Looks as if someone broke in at the back, came through the house and opened the front door from inside. Started up the stairs, and . . . after that, the deluge."

"Who would break in?"

"I don't know." His sharp eyes surveyed me. "There was a

quaint little advertisement in the newspaper a day or two ago. About the Kolumbe Nature Quiz. You see it?"

"Yes."

"Well, whoever put that advert in, has a lot to answer for."

He set down the glass with a bang and walked out of the room. I followed. Out on the lawn, was a group of people, Nick Corbitt, and Nell, a Captain of Police and a Leading Fireman. Nick's voice, high and wavering, carried across to me quite clearly.

⑤ ⑤ ⑤

XX

"I TELL YOU, it's my house and I'll enter it as and when I please!"

"Not unless we say so, sir." The fireman facing Nick was red-faced and sweating and looked as if he was going to grab Nick by the lapel any moment. "We have to get your sister out, and we'll do it faster if you let us get on with the job."

"Get out of my way!" Nick started forward and the police captain stepped into his path. He was a stocky man, past middle age, with a lot of muscle across the shoulders.

"Best to obey orders, Mr Corbitt." I thought there was a faintly sardonic note in the captain's voice.

"I am going in there." As I came closer I could see Nick's face, grey-green in the arc-lights, the lips drawn back almost as if he was having some sort of fit.

"As a good soldier, you know better. The firemen have work to do, let 'em get on with it."

"Keep your bloody advice to yourself. No one is going to keep me out of my own house."

"I am, sir, if that's the only way to save your neck." The policeman's eyes had taken on a pale glitter. "There are five men busy in there, and your sister may still be alive. You go stepping where it's not safe, and you can cause another slide that will kill her and the men too. So until the fire brigade gives the word, we'll all stay outside."

"You're exceeding your duty. I'll report you. What's your name?"

"Tebbutt. Arthur Tebbutt. Perhaps you'd remember me as Sergeant Tebbutt, Second Anti-Tank? I've seen your sort of courage too often, Mr Corbitt."

"Major!"

"Major Corbitt. And if I remember rightly, the last break you organised, twenty-seven of the boys never got past the wire in time. They're not handing out any medals in this operation, sir, and you'll stay out here on the lawn like I say."

Tebbutt turned abruptly away and walked towards the house with the fireman. Nick swung up an arm in a gesture of childish fury that brought Nell quickly to his side.

"No, Nick. The man's right. You have to think of Gretha, if she is alive."

"Gretha? Dead or alive, they have to find her, don't they? I should be helping in the search. What will people think if they hear that while other men risked their lives, I was safely on the terrace?"

"They will think you acted like a sensible man. The firemen are skilled, Nick, and you aren't. Besides, you can't lift a thing with those hands."

He thrust aside her soothing arm. "Derek says there's a window broken at the back. Who did that? That person is still in the house, probably? You thought of that?"

"I have, and there's nothing we can do about it. Perhaps the window was broken in the landslide. Nick, you must calm down. People are watching you." As she spoke, Nell was edging him back to the wheelchair on the grass; easing him down into it and spreading a rug over his knees. "It's cold here. Let me take you back to the house. You know it's bad for you to be out in this damp."

"Leave me alone! Where's Cory, I want him."

"Didn't he come with you?"

"No. He wasn't with me this afternoon."

"But who drove you to Pinetown?"

"I never went. They 'phoned to say the gates weren't ready, so I went to the Royal Durban with Waite. We saw the first few couples come in, had a drink and he brought me home." Nick spoke in the sulky tone of a child caught at the jam-jar.

Nell started to say something to him in a low voice. He shook his head peevishly. And then someone inside the house suddenly let out a yell like a banshee.

It was just one wild shout, and then silence, and then a man appeared gabbling at the upper window. He almost fell through it and slithered down the ladder to the ground. The other men in the garden ran to him, Sharvey and Tebbutt and several others. They stood there talking for a moment, and then the Leading Fireman started up the ladder with Sharvey after him.

Nell said, "They've found her." She wrapped her arms round herself and stood shivering, gazing up at the windows. Behind me Nick Corbitt sat completely still.

Sharvey reached the top of the ladder and ducked over the sill. There was an endless wait before he reappeared. He paused and then came down the ladder clumsily. He made his way past the tumbled hedge and stopped in front of Nell, his face screwed up in something part relief and part horror.

"It's not Gretha," he said.

Nell swayed forward, her arms still hugging her chest, and Sharvey caught her and thrust a hand under her jaw so that she had to look at him. "It's Cory," he told her. "Cory Bergen."

Just above a whisper she said, "He's dead?"

"Oh, Christ, yes. His head was torn clean off."

It was then that Nick began to scream. He sat in his wheelchair like a shrunken old puppet and from the round black hole of his mouth there came this high, agonised, animal shriek.

It was more than I could stand. I spun round and ran down

the drive as fast as I could, out of that damned garden and through the teak gates and straight into the mob that waited beyond them.

☙ ☙ ☙

XXI

HANDS SNATCHED AT me, faces thrust forward, voices shrilled and buzzed round my head, "Is she alive, did they get her out yet, what's happening?" I tried to force my way through, but the human pack-ice merely tightened its grip.

I panicked. I began to lash out with both fists. My knuckles squished against someone's nose and blood spurted. My feet slipped and I started to fall. At that moment, a sinewy arm locked round my waist, a gnomish dome bobbed under my left elbow, and a voice said, "Keep pedalling, Lennie."

I did as I was bid; and slowly, in the wake of Evan's sharp tongue and sharper boot, I found myself towed free.

Some of the crowd still tried to follow, skirmishing right to the end of the Crescent, where Evan's car waited in the nimbus of St. Michael and All Angels. Evan shoved me into the passenger seat and slammed the door, and then we were off, roaring round into Peak Road in top gear.

After that we seemed to drive in circles, very fast. Evan kept peering in the driving-mirror and swearing. After a while he grunted, slowed down, and turned through an archway into a courtyard. On the far side a neon sign blinked on and off, BAR LOUNGE.

I looked at Evan. "I can't go in there."

"Yes you can. Lights, and a load of Scotch is what we need. Come on."

He didn't speak again until the whisky and ice were set before us. Then he said, "Well, girl, start telling."

"They found Cory Bergen dead in the house." My teeth started to chatter on the rim of my glass. "His head's torn off. That's what Derek Sharvey said, and then Nick screamed. You can't imagine what it was like."

Evan reached over and took a firm hold on my wrist. "Don't hurry it, child. Go back a bit. Begin after the dinner at the Swordfish and work through."

At first my mind kept stalling and back-tracking, but then I calmed down and the events fell into the proper order. By the time I got to the conversation with Johan Dessels, I'd stopped shaking. Evan just sat and listened without saying a word, until I repeated what Sharvey had said, that whoever put the advertisement in the newspaper had a lot to answer for. Then he said, "No, that's nonsense. If you hadn't acted, someone else would. The truth is, Lennie, we're not the initiators in this. We've stumbled into someone else's little game, we can't blow the whistle, all we can do is play for our lives."

"You do agree, there is something horrible?"

"Yes, I agree. I didn't at first, now I do." He paused a moment, then went on, "The thing is, what are we to do about it? Who precisely did you speak to up at the Corbitt's? Nick and Nell, Sharvey, one of the firemen. Anyone else?"

"No."

"Police, press?"

"No, but they must have seen me there."

He nodded. "It's quite clear that Nell invited you over to warn you to keep your mouth shut about Kate."

"I think so."

"In the circumstances, she's probably right. You see, if we report our suspicions to the police, then one of two results will ensue. Either they will disbelieve us, in which case we don't help ourselves at all, either from the viewpoint of physical safety, or of discovering the truth. Or they will believe us, in which case they won't rest until they've learned everything we know, including your visit to Gretha's flat, and your putting in that advertisement. If we cry murder, then we can't expect to be left out of the hunt. It's our duty to go to the police, academically speaking, but I don't think we will. Would you like another drink?"

I nodded. I was thinking that I was never going to understand the oldies. I'd been ready for Evan to read me a lecture and rush for the fuzz. Instead, here he was plying me with drink and conspiring to conceal evidence. It struck me that we were only part of his reason. It was becoming pretty clear that my sainted aunt had been mixed up with some king-sized crooks, and Evan didn't want that made public. One thing I was sure of, he'd loved Kate in his own cranky way.

The second whisky began to melt the ice in my spine. I sipped it and said, "The police will suspect one crime at least. Attempted housebreaking. With a window forced at the back and the front door unlocked."

"It's possible Gretha forgot to lock up, for once."

"It's unheard of. The neighbours will tell how nobody goes in, no tradesmen, no one. All her groceries go through the hatch from the supermarket."

"Well, that may be to our advantage. A recluse like Gretha is usually suspected of concealing valuables in her mattress. That could provide a man like Bergen with a motive for breaking in."

"Why would he open the front door?"

"To provide an escape route if necessary. Then he could have started up the stairs and got pinned by a deadfall. Yes, the police may well think that's what happened."

"How do you think he came to be in the house?"

"One of two reasons. He was ordered in, or he was paid to go in."

"He took orders from Nick."

"A man like Bergen is for sale if the price is right." Evan looked at me thoughtfully. "If he was bought, then the buyer is still at large. So I won't have you living alone in that flat,

Lennie. You'd best come to me. Bertha will see to your comfort and you can come and go as you please."

"Thanks, Evan." Through the reaction and the whisky I was beginning to feel dopey. Thoughts drifted past me and I couldn't be bothered to pin them down. I said lazily, "I think Nick Corbitt's a queer."

"What makes you say so?"

"Don't know, exactly. This afternoon, up there, he didn't seem to give a damn about Gretha being trapped under all that lumber. He was worried about what people would think if he didn't form part of the rescue party. But when he found Cory Bergen was missing, he was suddenly scared stiff. And then Sharvey said they'd found Bergen, and Nick was hysterical. I think Bergen meant far more to him than his own sister."

"That doesn't make him a homosexual. Cory was with Nick for a quarter of a century, you know. Through the war and after. Lately Nick hasn't been able to dress himself or get out of a wheelchair without Cory's help. Cory was the guy who gave Nick his injections, went everywhere with him, looked after his business journeys, in fact kept him alive. That sort of total dependence must include emotional dependence, surely?

"I admit Nick was always a bit too good-looking to be true. You know the sort, always has a cluster of women around, likes the hunt but never seems to move in for the kill? Almost sexless, in the way a young god is sexless. Baldur the Beautiful."

"A peacock," I said, and Evan nodded.

"Exactly. Kate chose the right symbol for him. When Nick was a kid, there were too many adoring relations, encouraging him to stalk and preen. I thought the war might bring him down to earth but it didn't. He dropped one plane only, from god to hero."

"There was a police officer today, a Captain Tebbutt, who said something about Nick's heroism. I don't think he liked Nick, more or less suggested he won medals by risking other men's lives."

"That's unjust. Nick organised prison-breaks. P.O.W.'s are supposed to escape if they can, Nick ran severe risks and spent a long time in solitary confinement. That's what started the arthritic trouble. The poor guy's had hell for twenty years, I suppose one shouldn't grudge him his dusty laurels. Bergen, though, there was nothing heroic about him. He was never anything more than a professional thug. "Killer" Bergen, they called him. He was middle-weight champion of the Army at one time; went into the bag with Nick, became his right-hand man, stood over his near-corpse when hostilities ended, and has battened on the Corbitts ever since. Cory lived ... well, not like a prince, but certainly like a Grand Vizier."

"Why did Nell allow it?"

"Couldn't prevent it, I'd say. Nick was utterly dependent on Cory for some time."

"You don't think he had some hold over the Corbitts? For instance, if he knew something about Gretha?"

"It's possible. Bergen was a bad creature when I knew him and I don't imagine he improved with age. Well, he's dead now, and no one will mourn him, except Nick."

Evan sat musing for a while, and then shook his head. "You know, Lennie, one thing puzzles me, and that's the way that all these people hang together. They're like a lot of puppets with the strings tangled. Jerk one, they all react. On the surface they have nothing in common, yet they protect one another. Do you notice that none of them has given us any information about the others invited to Kate's party? It's almost as if they've made a pact of silence."

He held up a hand and began to tick off fingers. "There were twelve people invited to Kate's party. We already know, or think we know, nine of them. Nell and Derek Sharvey, Nick and Gretha Corbitt, Ralph Bryant, Johan Dessels, Jean-Paul Greco, and Cory Bergen. Then there's the Mr Silke that Dessels mentioned."

"And Percy Kennedy," I said. "Does the name ring any bells with you?"

"Can't say it does. It's not exactly distinctive, though."

"This meeting with his sister, tomorrow. Could you come with me?"

He considered. "I think it'd be better if I eavesdropped. We'll get there early and Georgy can arrange to hide me somewhere."

"I wondered," I said, "if I should ask Dave to hang about and try and get a picture of the lady?"

Evan looked at me unhappily. "You mustn't rely on Leatherhead. He's Greco's stepson and I'm not at all sure he's not acting as Greco's agent."

"He loathes Greco."

"So he says, but he could be lying. He's lied about other things. No, don't bristle up. I've been making some enquiries. Yesterday morning I went round to Chopping and Spicer's. You'll be interested to hear that Leatherhead isn't retained by them. They expressed surprise that he should be taking photographs on the Peak Hill site. Then, when I left, I nearly bumped into Leatherhead, in the company of Derek Sharvey."

"Sharvey!?"

"Yes. There was no mistake. The two of them came up the steps from the street, as I came out of the door. I ducked back and they never saw me, although they passed quite close. Leatherhead was doing some fast talking by the look of it, and Sharvey was listening, and they didn't look like chance acquaintances. So why didn't Dave tell us he knew Sharvey?"

"Perhaps it's recent. Perhaps he's interested in Sharvey, and thinks he put the article in the *Chronicle*, and wants to check up. You can't assume they're in cahoots just because you see them talking to each other."

"Lennie, face facts. The evening you met him, David Leatherhead was up on Peak Hill taking photographs of the area where Sharvey lives. When Sharvey heard that, on your own report he sounded startled and concerned. Furthermore Leatherhead lied to you about his occupation. You can't trust him."

"Come to that, why should he trust us? To him, we are people mixed up with the Corbitts and the Sharveys. He's taking us at our word, all the same. He likes us."

"And you like him?"

"Yes." I was angry with Evan, but I knew he was justified. I liked Dave instinctively, because of something in him, the things he liked doing, such as taking a picture of the Pel's fishing-owl.

But I also knew he wasn't telling me the whole truth about himself.
I said, "Innocent until proved guilty."

Evan grunted, but didn't go on about it. He got up from his
chair. "Home."

"Fine, but can I call at the flat on the way? I'd like to get
some clothes."

He drove me across and went up to the flat with me. I packed
a suitcase and included the box of Hallowe'en favours.

Back at Evan's, I was given a huge nursery supper by old
Bertha, his housekeeper who's known me for ever. Then I had a
bath and climbed into bed; yet although I was dead weary, I
couldn't sleep. I kept thinking about Gretha Corbitt, and how
the fireman had said it would be better if she were dead than
lying injured under the junk. I wondered how long it would take
to reach her and Lorca. I thought about Nick and Nell Corbitt.
Had they quieted Nick? A peacock, vain and shrill, and past
beauty. Kate had been harsh in her judgement of her friends.
Bergen she knew as a shrike. Nell, the owl. That was wisdom,
wasn't it, or magic? The owl was a bird of prey, a hunter,
floating silent above the moon-blue Kolumbe estuary.

Kate knew ... Kate knew ...? For a moment I almost felt I
shared her knowledge, but then I sank a sea mile deep in sleep.

XXII

NEXT MORNING, WHEN I went down to breakfast at
seven, Evan was already at the table, reading the newspaper.
He handed it across to me.

"In full cry," he said.

The Corbitt thing was second lead on the front page. There was a picture of the fallen façade with firemen working over it, and an inset picture of Cory Bergen. The caption to that gave details of his Army career. The police were said to be working on the theory that Mr Bergen, who was once a notable middle-weight boxer, entered the house to apprehend an intruder who forced a window at the back. It was believed that a collapse of debris ensued, which killed Mr Bergen instantaneously. The Chief of Police issued a severe warning to householders who stored rubbish to the extent that it constituted a hazard to human life.

The Fire Brigade stated that there might be more victims trapped in the lower part of the house. Miss Gretha Corbitt, the owner, and her white Alsatian dog, were missing, and every effort was being made to reach them as quickly as possible. However, it was feared that total clearance might take as long as forty-eight hours. Debris must be moved carefully to avoid causing further slides, and the stairway itself was sagging dangerously, and must be shored up. A Mr Cameron Luyt, who had worked on bombed houses during World War II, was being flown from Johannesburg to direct operations, and medical men were standing by to render assistance where needed.

Neither Mrs Nell Sharvey, the missing woman's sister, nor her brother Mr Nick Corbitt, was available for comment, as they were still in a state of shock, but Mr Derek Sharvey had said that Miss Corbitt was an eccentric who ignored all her family's pleas about keeping the building clear of rubbish, and who steadfastly refused to let anyone handle her affairs for her. (I thought that was smart of Sharvey. It suggested Gretha was a stubborn nut, but not so nutty that she couldn't bear the blame for what had happened.)

The reporter had talked to a number of people in the crowd in Michael Crescent. One of these, a cashier from the Peak Hill shopping centre, said it was a downright shame that a poor sick lady like Miss Corbitt should be allowed to live that way, and there ought to be a law against it.

On page fourteen the paper ran a feature article on Michael Crescent. "Luckless" and "jinxed" were two of the adjectives used, and there was a three-column rehash of the Kate Falconer enigma.

So much for keeping things quiet.

I looked at Evan. "They're going to hunt for the connection."

"Yes, I'm afraid so. Whoever started all this must be feeling pretty pleased with himself." He drank some of his coffee. "Unless, of course, your theory is right and it was Gretha."

"I'm sure it was."

"Well, this last catastrophe seems to support your idea. After all, why break into her flat unless it was to stop her handing out any further information? Poor woman, she got more than she bargained for. Well, now she's gone, it may be the whole thing will fade."

"No. We can't let it."

"Now, Lennie . . ."

"It's no good, Evan. I talked to Gretha. She needed my help. She gave me the favours because in some crazy way she trusted me to try and find out what happened to Kate. That's what she wanted. It'd be a grotty deal if I opted out now. Anyway, Kate was my blood relation."

"You don't need to remind me." His voice was bitter. "You're too damn like her. I've seen her in you, time and again, and I want to tell you something. It's not just your conscience that's driving you now, it's your taste for danger. Danger smiles, and you follow. It's a family trait, it killed Kate, so take care." He rose abruptly from the table. "Come, finish your coffee. We'll be late."

The Hurly Burly is a restaurant in the old Hudson Hotel, which backs on to Albert Park. It's close enough to the Bay to get the smell of mud at low tide, but not close enough to have a Bay view. Until Georgy Micklebust took it over, it was a dead dull place for up-country farmers and their wives. Georgy arrived from Manchester, fixed the Hudson's roof and plumbing, and knocked out practically the whole of the back wall on the top floor. That opened up a tremendous view, right across the park, the bayhead, and up the slope of the Berea to the University. Georgy placed the Hurly Burly there, went for good tropical dishes and imported entertainers. In the evening the crowd is mostly young executives, but during the day it's just bayside residents and sailing people who enjoy the food. At ten to eight, when we walked in, there were a couple of dozen having breakfast.

Georgy came over, asked how I was and swapped a bit of fishing gossip with Evan. But when he started to lead us to a table by the window, Evan stopped him.

"Leonora will sit here, but I'd like a spot where I can see unseen."

Georgy bowed without comment, hid Evan behind a bank of outsize plastic orchids, and gave me a table near the door. As I sat down I said, "Georgy, do you know a Miss Lola Kennedy?"

He shook his head, his face blank but his bootbutton eyes inquisitive.

"Would you mind taking a look at the woman I'm meeting? See if you or the waiters recognise her?"

"Certainly."

I ordered coffee and sat sipping and watching the door. I swear I never shifted my gaze, but I never saw Lola arrive. One moment there was no one and the next, there she was, like a chameleon that's been waiting on the branch all the time.

She was pale, that was the word that sprang to my mind. Dumpy and pale, with freckles. Her head was bare and her sandy hair was cut very short so I could see the thick pale neck. I shouldn't think she'd changed her hair style since 1930. It was docked straight across, parted and clipped back on one side with a child's tortoiseshell slide. She wore a crumpled cotton dress, reddish and speckled like dried orange peel, and the V of exposed chest was speckled too. In one hand was an orange plastic handbag, the other cupped a cigarette, turning it inwards as a Moslem does. She lifted it and took a quick furtive puff and I saw the brown stain along the side of her palm where the smoke must always curl out. Then she caught sight of me, stared a moment, and came over.

I held out my hand. The grasp that enclosed it was cold and sliding. The woman flopped down in the chair opposite me and her body went soft, the breasts and stomach and flabby upper arms melding into one mass. My first thought was, we'd boobed, this was just the sort of seedy housewife who'd think it smart to lay claim to a prize that wasn't hers. Then I saw her eyes. They were mean eyes, wet and green as lime drops, eyes that had done a lot of cheating; but they were also scared. They recognised me and for some reason I scared them witless. It was a very brief impression. The heavy eyelids drooped, a pale hand swung the handbag to the table, pale lips spread in a gat-toothed smile.

I said, "I'm Leonora Bryant."

"Lola Kennedy." It was the same voice I'd heard on the telephone, husky and flat.

"Would you like tea or coffee?"

"Nothing. I can't stay." She opened the bag and took out a sheaf of papers, passed them across to me. An identity card was clipped to the top. Her features were no more fetching under mica. There were two other documents, a letter signed by Percy Kennedy introducing his sister Miss Lola Kennedy of the Gloriana Café, Point Road, Durban; and a power of attorney authorising the said Miss Kennedy to stick her ugly fingers into Mr Percy's monetary affairs any time she liked. A covering letter showed that the power of attorney had been drawn up by a reputable firm of lawyers.

I looked the papers over carefully and then said, "They seem perfectly in order, Miss Kennedy. I'll hand them over to my Committee and I've no doubt they'll make payment in due course."

I reached for the check on the tray. Everything depended on her next move, whether she accepted what I said, showing she was interested only in the money, or whether she'd try to detain me and find out what my angle was.

Her hand darted forward, pinning down the check. "Wait. It's not that easy, Miss Bryant."

"I beg your pardon?"

"I want to know what you're buying for a hundred rand. There's no Kolumbe Quiz. Never has been. So why'd you put that ad in?"

"I'm afraid I don't understand." I put all the starch into it I could, hoping to goad her, and I did. Her mouth took on a decidedly nasty line.

"Listen, maybe I should take what I know elsewhere. Maybe I should go'n have a yak with Mr Sharvey."

"By all means, although at the moment the Sharveys have enough trouble."

I stood up firmly. So did Lola, pulling her soft mass upright with surprising speed. There was an unpleasant smell about her, not unclean so much as unhealthy, musty. She said, "How did you know Percy was Mynah?"

I made no answer and the green eyes leaned closer. "You're Kate's niece. Who told you about Mynah?"

I shook my head. "Did you know my aunt Kate, Miss Kennedy?"

She stared at me, uncertain, and then a malicious grin touched her mouth. "Who me? Kate was hardly the Point Road type, was she?"

"Nor were you, once."

The grin vanished. "Okay, Miss Bryant, let's cut out the clever bit. You're offering a hundred rand, and that'd be something nice in the kitty, but I told you, we want to know what you expect for your money. Fair enough, isn' it?"

"Fair enough. I'll explain it all to Mynah himself. Not to anyone else."

She thought about that. "Come to the café. I'll bring him."

"No. Too public."

Again I caught a glimpse of panic, quickly suppressed. She said unwillingly. "All right. You can come to the house. Tonight. You come alone, though."

"I shall bring a companion."

"Listen, don't push your luck."

"What's the address?"

Sullenly she answered, "597 Syringa Park Road, Mobeni."

"We'll find it. What time?"

"Eight, nine. We'll be home."

"Au revoir, Miss Kennedy."

She gave me one more baleful glance, picked up the orange purse and made for the door. I sat down again and waited for Evan. He bounced out from behind his screen with gleeful speed.

"You got her rattled, love, and I've news for you. The name may be Kennedy now, but it used to be Kandell."

"You've met her before?"

"No, her brother. The family likeness is striking. There was a Paul Kandell who did some work for Sidney Falconer. A complete tit. God knows how he ever got invited to Kate's party, I wouldn't have thought they had anything in common."

"Could we find out anything more about him, do you think, before we see him tonight?"

Evan pulled at his lip. "We could ask Tim Mulvaney. If Paul Kandell changed his name, it was probably for police reasons. Tim may remember something. I'll 'phone him right away."

XXIII

T IM SAID, GIVE him the morning to ask around, and he'd see us at his house about two o'clock. Tim retired from the police a few years ago, and runs a private enquiry agency, but his chief asset is his memory. He can remember everything that happened in any major rugby game over thirty years, and his mental index of crime and criminals is just as accurate.

Tim's grandfather was Irish and his grandmother half Hungarian and half Cape Coloured, although that's not admitted in polite circles. If you know a better pedigree for a drinking man, I don't. He's over sixty years old, with thick curling grey hair cropped very close to an angular skull. His skin is pocked like a dead planet. It's only when you look at his eyes, long and bright blue and glinting, that you can see why the girls have always loved him.

When we walked through his gate, he was working in the garden. He tied up a length of some yellow creeper, and led us over to the shade of a big old lychee tree, where three rickety cane chairs waited.

When we were settled, he said, "This bugger you mentioned, Kandell. Officially, there's nothing on him."

"Yet he changed his name," said Evan.

"Foreigner for a dad," said Tim, but added, "you're right, though, he wanted to get lost a while. Take a look at this." He handed over a newspaper cutting, a photograph showing a man and woman walking down a flight of stone steps. One was Lola, the other, Mr Paul Kandell.

"Central Criminal Court," said Tim. "They sat in the public gallery. They should've been in the dock. Bloody cheek, they had."

We waited while his inward eye brooded on old history. At length he said, "They never had cause to live like they did. Their old man was decent, came from Czechoslovakia before the war, a chemist and did well. Got a job on the research side of

Probyn's Brick and Tile, married and had these two kids. He kept things nice at home and Paul went to University, got a B.Sc., and followed his dad into Probyn's. By 1946, that's the date you asked me to check, he was a top analyst, and set fair, Probyn's being one of our biggest industries as you know. But Paul was the sort of clot that never thinks he's getting enough. In 1948 Probyn's found someone was selling information about their processes. They called in the police. No charge was brought, but Kandell left the firm. After that he sailed very close to the wind. Ran a racket that sold coloured water to Africans at five bob a bottle. Took up with a couple of okes that we suspected of doping race-horses. Then it was land deals that smelled nasty. But what nearly fixed him was *dagga*. There was this gang running the leaf up from the Transkei, used a fleet of African taxis. Here, it was flogged to Indians who passed it to seamen and the local blacks. Kids didn't smoke pot in those days, but it was always big money. We never pinned anything on Kandell, but he was close enough to singe his eyebrows, and when the trials were over, he quit Durban. Went to Jo'burg and changed his name by deed poll, to Percy Kennedy. A few years later he was back at the coast, smooth as milk. Bought a house at Mobeni and settled down. Income secure, reformed character by all accounts. Travelled a good deal, going all over the Republic, and up to Mozambique and Rhodesia. And you know what his job was? Preacher. Ja, I thought you'd like that. Percy Kennedy is the dominee of a phoney church with visiting missioners and a shiny little magazine once a month, and a bit of religion from every ragbag in the world. We checked Paul-Percy pretty carefully, but there's no law against seeing the light your own way. There's plenty of decent people will tell you Percy's saved them from damnation. God moves in a mysterious way, eh? But we'll get Percy one day. Know why? Because the church is a cover. He lives the way no genuine preacher can afford to live, and the money's not earned right, we're sure of that.

"See, the members of Percy's congregations ... he's got a set-up in every big city and port and in the mining towns too ... they're the sort of person who doesn't buy the big, stable religions. You know what that means? A lot of them are the sort a con man prays to meet. Lonely widows that want to send messages to their hubbies in heaven, alcoholics and queers and cranks that like religion syruped up so they can't taste the brimstone. And a lot of them are also nicely placed in industry and commerce, where they can pick up the sort of info a smartie like Percy can use. Things like what new processes are being developed, which company's got money troubles, who's taking on extra help and who's got a fight in the Director's suite.

"Percy Kandell has built up an organisation like a big sponge. He can squeeze enough out of it to sell to the takeover boys. In other words, he's back at his first game, industrial spying, but he doesn't take the risks and he only sells to the highest bidders. He keeps out of the public eye and lives like a fighting cock. Must be in the early sixties now, and no one can say his crimes don't pay.

"You asked about his sister. Lola Kandell, now Kennedy. She never had much between the ears. Went to a good school but straight after began to slide. It's my bet she pulled her brother down with her. She's not a nice girl. Twenty years ago she already ran a dance club that came close to being a brothel. She was in all Percy's rackets. Now he's a preacher she keeps house for him, but she still collects the rents for a couple of cafés she owns down in Point Road.

"Then there's one last member of the family you won't know about. Percy produced an illegitimate daughter when he was a lad. Doted on the kid. The one decent thing he ever did was look after her, sent her to a convent school, and after that to some posh place in Switzerland. She was there during the war and came home to Durban after, but maybe she's got too good for her dad because in 1947 she pushed off to the Transvaal and nobody seems to know what happened to her after."

"What was her name?"

"Hilary." Tim's bright eyes watched me thoughtfully, and I could see he was dying to ask what my angle was. But the friend triumphed over the policeman in him, and he merely said, "I hope I've given you what you need, Lennie."

"Thanks, Tim, you've been wonderful."

"Don't try and do anything silly, now, girl."

"I won't do anything you wouldn't do, Tim."

He grimaced, and grinned, and walked us to the gate. As I climbed into the car, Evan said, "Hilary Kandell, H.K., the Cuckoo."

I nodded. "Ten up and two to go."

⑨ ⑨ ⑨

XXIV

"Ten and a half," said Evan, as we headed for home, "if you include the Morty Silke that Johan Dessels mentioned." He swung the car round a milk lorry. "I never heard of this Hilary Kandell, but that's hardly surprising if she was illegitimate."

My mind was on a different tack. "If Hilary lived in Europe during the war, it's possible she knew Greco."

"It is, and also that she introduced him to her father back in Durban. Everything points to the fact that Percy was on the skids before 1946 when he knew Kate. I wouldn't be surprised if he was trying to work a scheme with one of the other people invited to that party."

"Derek Sharvey, perhaps."

"More likely to be Greco, or this Silke fellow, or the I.H. we haven't identified. One thing's proven, Lennie. Kate's guest list included a number of people who didn't belong round a polite dinner table."

"So she never meant it to be a polite dinner?"

"Precisely. What Kate planned for the night of October 31st wasn't a party, but a showdown. On October 30th someone took

127

steps to prevent it happening. Kate was silenced. We'll never know the reason, because Kate can't tell us, and the guilty person won't."

We drove in silence for a while. Heavy rain clouds were coming in from the sea to the southwest, and the air was torpid, as if even the weather was trying to muffle speech and thought; and yet I knew we were close to the truth, it was there if only we could recognise it.

"It's Michael Crescent," I said, "something about the Crescent. That's where it started." Evan shook his head vaguely and the thin thread of an idea slipped away from me. I groped for it again.

"You said a showdown. All this week I've been wondering what brought such unsuitable people together, and one answer is a dispute, isn't it? If they were involved in a dispute about money, or property, they'd meet? Each of them was short of money at that time.

"My own father was in difficulties, wasn't he? You say for years he'd talked of selling the house and land in the Crescent, and Nell and Kate and my mother persuaded him not to. After my mother died, he talked again about selling. What if Percy's scheme was to buy the ground and build the supermarket? Even in those days, five acres of land was worth a lot."

"Not enough to attract a crook like Greco. He wouldn't want to sit about while the land was acquired and plans passed for development."

"He might have meant to buy cheap from my father on a forced sale, and then sell at a good profit to a developing company. Dave told us he was in trouble at the time, on the run from Europe and needing sterling. What if he decided Michael Crescent was a good prospect? Perhaps he used Percy as an approach to the Falconers. Perhaps Derek Sharvey helped. Kandell was in the same line of business, in a way. He worked at Probyn's Brick and Tile, and my father and Sharvey dealt in building materials. They might easily have known each other. Kandell could easily have worked out some deal with my father as fall guy. He was always easy to fool. Look at the emblem Kate chose for him, a turkey. What do you do with a turkey but fatten it for the kill?

128

"Let's suppose my father was being conned into selling the Falconer estate for some ridiculous amount, and Kate found out about it. Mightn't she plan a showdown, to prove to my father he was being done? Doesn't it explain why she invited two groups that seemed to have nothing in common with each other: Greco's clique, and her own group of friends who she knew would back her up in opposing the sale?

"What if Greco found out what Kate was up to? Mightn't he decide to put her out of his way? So Kate suffered an accident, there was no party, no exposure, my father sold the house. The Corbitts raised hell about that, but they couldn't stop the sale.

"My father left town and went to the farm and that might have been the end of it but for one thing. Gretha Corbitt knew what happened to Kate, she actually saw her body. Luckily for the killer, nobody believed her story. Her own sister was so scared that Gretha would be locked in an asylum, that she coaxed or bullied her into silence. For twenty years Gretha lived in almost total isolation. Fact and fiction were all muddled up in her mind. But for some reason, this year, her memory started to come back. She wanted to break out of her prison, but she had no one to help her do it. She sent an anonymous draft to the *Chronicle*, hinting at the old Kate Falconer scandal. It was printed. One of the people concerned guessed who'd sent it, and tried to silence her as he'd silenced Kate. It fits, doesn't it, Evan?"

"Almost," he said, "but not quite. You say the party was cancelled because Kate vanished. But Kate herself told Ralph, on October 30th before she left home, that the party was off. And if your explanation is correct, where do Cory Bergen and Johan Dessels fit in? Why were they invited to the party?"

"Dessels because he was Kate's trusted friend. Bergen because he was in Nick's employ and would do as he was told, but perhaps also because as an ex-pug he could be useful if there was any rough stuff."

Evan shook his head. "It's possible, I suppose, but it doesn't satisfy me. It's too ... small. Greco wouldn't risk murder for five acres of land, and I don't think Kandell would risk it at all."

"They could have paid Bergen."

"Yes, but ... the whole thing is preposterous. If I found a gang of sharpies was trying to fiddle me, I wouldn't invite them to a party, I'd invite them to my office and make sure I had a bloody good lawyer waiting for them."

"Of course you would, and so would most people, but not Kate. Kate would choose a way that allowed her to make her own judgement and fix her own punishment. That's why she didn't invite you, Evan darling."

I knew what I said was true. I knew because at that moment, Kate possessed my mind. My home was in Michael Crescent. My friends were the Corbitts next door, and my enemies the people who had tried to cheat me out of my inheritance.

I glanced at Evan and found him staring at me with doubt and a sort of horror. He said, "Lennie, it's not for us to exact vengeance. You don't know . . ."

But a car behind us hooted, Evan's gaze jerked back to the road ahead, and the sentence was never finished. We reached the gates of his house and turned through them. The pine-trees on the Ridge flickered with blue-green light, and vanished in a tumult of rain. We tumbled out of the car and sprinted for the shelter of the front porch.

$$\mathcal{S} \quad \mathcal{S} \quad \mathcal{S}$$

XXV

BY THE TIME we'd finished dinner, the sky was clear, but a cold wind was still blowing from the south. Evan and I drove out of town, past the power station and the flour factory to the main factory area of Mobeni. Then we got lost, looking for Syringa

Park Road. It was after eight-thirty when we found it, and reached the Kennedy house. This was one of those red brick boxes on a quarter-acre plot with a nice view of the glue factory. I reckon a glue-sniffer could get high there any week-night, just by holding his breath.

We parked the car a little up the road, and walked back along a tall wire mesh fence that bordered two or three small vacant sites. The Kennedy house had no garden to speak of, just a couple of diseased aloes and some stunted hydrangea bushes.

Evan pushed open double gates and we went up a sandy drive. At the top was a yard with a couple of sheds with rickety doors that didn't quite shut. We picked our way over to the house. The lower brickwork was splashed with mud from the stormdrains. A path led round to the front door. There was a bow window to the left of the door and as we passed its tightly-drawn curtains I could hear a radio going inside, and someone talking above that. The voice sounded angry.

We marched up the front steps. Evan raised his fist and thumped the door twice. The angry voice stopped and out of the tail of my eye I saw the curtains at the window twitch. A moment or two later, the door opened, and Titania of Point Road stood there, piggy eyes, freckles and all. A cigarette drooped between her lips and she squinted at Evan past a curl of smoke.

I said, "This is Dr Evan Cruikshank." Evan ducked his head and said "Good evening," and the woman stepped back and let us in. We followed her along the passage and sharp left into the pastor's living-room.

It was huge, crowded and tasteless. It looked as if everything in it had been bought in one burst at one shop. Yet it had cost a lot of money. The embossed carpet, the Dralon chair-seats, the Hi-Fi in the corner, were all of superb quality. Maybe they acquired their natty look from living too close to Percy. There was a niche in the wall opposite the door and in it stood a pair of candles, a Bible and a bowl of flowers.

Percy was standing beside this niche in a thoughtful attitude, but as we entered he turned and surged across the floor with hands held high, as if he meant to lead us into a *pas de trois*. He was tall and pudgy. When he greeted me I looked up at a replica of Lola's face, the same pale speckled skin, sandy hair smoothed back from a central parting, small green eyes between puffy lids. The likeness was superficial, though. Where Lola was stolid, Percy was excessively mobile. His lips curled and budded over pink shiny gums, his nose twitched, his eyes continually widened and narrowed and even the skin of his scalp rippled back and forth until I thought it might slide right off his skull. He was neatly dressed in a fawn Trevira suit, brown shirt and Batik tie. His voice when it came was thick yet fluting.

"A pleasure to meet you, Miss Bryant."

"And you, Mr Kandell."

A plump hand wagged at me. "Kennedy, please Miss Bryant, the name is Kennedy. The past is over and done with. Take a seat, won't you? Over here, is that comfortable? And Dr Cruikshank, here? What can I offer you, whisky, beer, coffee and liqueur? It's all ready waiting?"

I settled for black coffee, Evan for brandy and water. Percy poured himself a Tia Maria and took the upright chair between us. With a flash of gums he said, "Easier to talk, isn't it, with a glass or a cup in hand? I find that with my People. Truth in the flask, whether it be wine or weak tea. And truth is what we all seek, isn't that so? It's clear to me, Doctor and Miss Bryant, that you, like myself, are anxious to attain the truth. Facts, facts is what we need. That's why you put that advertisement in the paper, because you want facts; answers to certain questions that trouble the heart and cloud the clear spirit. Well, here we are, Lola and I, ready to provide what answers we can, and hoping that you in your turn will try to shed light on our dark places."

"My first question," I said, "is why did you send your sister to meet me instead of coming yourself?"

He nodded several times. "That is easy. I sent Lola because I wanted to discover who you were. We're none of us kiddies any longer, we all know that the world is full of unscrupulous folk who lay traps for the unwary. In my profession I have to be jealous of my good name, very jealous. I mean, if I accepted money from a source that wasn't just so, the members of my flock would be down on me like a ton of bricks. Put it this way. I read your advert, Miss Bryant, and I thought, 'Now what's all this?

132

Why is someone offering a hundred rand to me as prize in a competition I never entered?' There's been no Kolumbe Nature Quiz, you know it and I know it. So my first question to you is, what is your reason for putting down hard cash, what are you after? Frankly, until I know what I'm selling, I'd rather not accept the cash. See what I mean?"

"Perfectly," said Evan, and got a smile that seemed to move Percy's scalp through ninety degrees.

"Can't be too careful. We're all business people, umh? I'm not a young man, Doctor, and I look forward to retiring soon. Eh, Lola? Peace at the end, Miss Bryant. So what do you want of us, name it, and if it's within our power to give satisfaction, we will, and close the matter. Eh?"

I looked at him. If you ignored those elastic features, you found that the eyes were cold and steady. I said, "I am the niece of Kate Falconer. In 1946, she planned to hold a party. I'm looking for the people she invited. You were one of them, Mr Kennedy."

"Kate Falconer. That's a long time ago, a very long time. I only met her in the business line, you know."

"As an employee of Probyn's Brick and Tile?"

"That is correct."

"You were working as an analyst."

"Yes, yes. Lots of new building materials were developed just after the war."

"And you did some special work for my grandfather, Sidney Falconer?"

"That's right. We provided a new type of tile for the roof at his farm. Blue, very pretty and hardwearing. I wouldn't be surprised to hear they're still in place."

"They are. Having worked with my grandfather, I suppose you got to know my father quite well?"

"We were in the same line, building materials. We met from time to time. A nice man, your dad, very easy-going."

"And my father's partner, Derek Sharvey?"

"Yes, I knew him. Not socially, mind."

At that, Lola burst into harsh laughter. "Socially! That's a joke. All Nell and Derek Sharvey cared about was money for that bloody house of theirs, they wouldn't talk to you unless you were sitting with your bum in the butter. As for Nick Corbitt, nobody with a name like Kandell had a chance with him. Him and his regimental band! If you ask me ..."

"But I don't. Live and let live, Lola dear." Percy's eyes carried such warning that his sister sank back in her chair. The rage died from her face and gave way to the old sullen glowering.

"Yes." Percy turned back to me. "Live and let live. That was the way it was between me and the Corbitts. We weren't friends, but we conducted our business on a friendly footing."

"And was that the way with my aunt Kate, too?"

"Pardon?"

"Why did Kate Falconer invite you to her Hallowe'en party, Mr Kennedy? Was it for business or pleasure?"

He pursed his lips. "A little of each, I daresay. Most likely I'd have talked business with your dad and the rest. In those days, my mind was on fleshly matters." He gazed soulfully at the niche in the wall.

"What about your daughter Hilary? Why was she invited?"

That was the first hit. Percy's scalp jerked and for a moment he looked scared. Then he shrugged. "Hilary came down suddenly from Jo'burg to stay with me. So I took her along."

It was obviously a lie, since Kate had known about her coming far enough in advance to design an emblem for her. I stared at Percy without saying anything and was glad to see sweat on his freckled forehead.

Evan suddenly intervened. "Tell me, Mr Kennedy, how well did you know Cory Bergen?"

Percy shook his head firmly. "Not at all."

"But you must have met him."

"Oh, perhaps once or twice, but he was nothing more than a high-grade servant, you know. He didn't mingle with the guests."

"He was invited to the Hallowe'en party."

"That's not my affair. I know nothing about Bergen."

"Just as well, since he's died in very awkward circumstances. The police are anxious to know why he went into Gretha Corbitt's apartment. Can you think of a reason?"

Percy leaned back in his chair and made no answer.

"My own view," Evan's eye had a bright innocence, "is that

Bergen was sent in. But who sent him? That, you might say, is the hundred rand question, Mr Kennedy. Who sent Cory Bergen into Gretha Corbitt's flat? If you can answer that question, the money is yours."

Percy stood up. "I don't want your bribes!" An extraordinary contortion of his face turned a snarl into an unctuous smirk. "I wish I could help you, for old time's sweet sake. I was fond of Kate Falconer and I'd be glad to help any relation of hers, but I'm afraid I know nothing about Bergen's affairs. I was never close to the Corbitts, and I haven't been near Michael Crescent in twenty years."

Evan pulled a roll of notes from his pocket and held them out to the silent Lola. "Miss Kennedy? How about you?" Lola's eyes looked wistful, but she shook her head. Evan turned back to Percy.

"Perhaps I should send them to Hilary? Maybe she knows the answer. What do you think?"

Colour surged up Percy's neck and he poked his head forward like a snapping turtle. "You leave my daughter out of this. She doesn't need your money, she could buy you out with one week's housekeeping." He checked and made a clicking sound with his tongue. "Dear me, I'm overwrought, aren't I? Forgive me, Dr Cruikshank. I'm afraid I'm weary. Just back from a long journey and the work is arduous. Yes, bringing souls to the light takes it out of you. I've been frank with you, more frank than you've been with me, but with the best will in the world, I can't answer your query, and nor can my sister or my daughter."

Still trying, I said, "Perhaps Mortimer Silke could?"

It was no good. Percy had himself under control. The smile he gave me was kind. "I'm sure not, Miss Bryant." He glanced thoughtfully at his fingernails. "Mr Silke is, like the rest of us, a seeker after truth. No doubt he would give much more than a hundred rand to find it, but truth is an elusive nymph, is she not? And now, if you'll forgive me, I must retire. I need solitude in the evenings, time to meditate and calm the vibrations of the spirit. I know you'll excuse me. Good night. Lola will see you out."

There was nothing we could do but accept dismissal. Lola let us out of the front door. As it closed after us, I heard music begin in the living-room, Dvorak I think, like water falling thinly from a high cliff. I said crossly, "That creature does nothing to calm my vibrations."

"No." Evan sounded distrait. "He smears all he touches, I should say."

Outside, the smell of glue was overpowering. It was pitch dark and the rain had started again, blurring the fence, the garden, and even the outline of the house. I started down the drive, but Evan to my surprise suddenly turned right and nipped towards the shed. I saw him wriggle through the doors. A minute later he reappeared, grabbed my arm and hustled me away. We reached the car, and climbed in. I felt draggled and depressed. "We didn't get a damn thing."

"Oh yes, we did." Evan was looking quietly smug. He concentrated on his driving until we were back on the main road, and then said:

"In the search for truth, as Percy probably does not appreciate, it's as important to collect the negative evidence as the positive. You've learned a good deal tonight. You know that Percy and Hilary Kandell were not friends of Kate's, yet she invited them both to her party. That supports your theory that the guests fell into two opposing groups. You've learned that Percy knew Morty Silke and probably is still in touch with him. You know that Percy spends far more money than he can possibly earn as a preacher in a phoney cult. If you need further proof of that, let me tell you that that ramshackle shed behind the house contains two brand new cars, a Fiat and a Mercedes Benz. The Mercedes is maroon. I've never seen that colour before, so either it's the newest model, or it's custom-finished."

A picture flashed across my mind and I said, "There was a maroon Mercedes on the roof of the Peak Hill Shopping Centre, the evening I met Dave Leatherhead."

"Then very possibly Mr Kandell was there, keeping an eye on Dave, or Michael Crescent, or both. You know Lennie, I've been thinking that whoever broke into Gretha Corbitt's flat, aside from Cory Bergen, must have had to study the ground quite thoroughly. One way to do that would be to climb to the top of the Shopping

Centre. The other way would be to take pictures from Peak Hill with a telescopic lens."

"If you're suggesting that Dave Leatherhead and Percy Kandell are working together then I don't believe it."

"Kandell knew Greco. Dave may be acting for Greco now."

"I don't believe it."

Evan sighed. "Anyway, I got the registration numbers of both cars." He pushed over a pocket diary. On the back page was scrawled,

Fiat   ND 001-10

Merc.   TJ 14372-331

"The Fiat is Durban registered and probably belongs to the Kennedy Kandells. The Mercedes is Transvaal, Johannesburg so they don't own it. It could be a company car, of course, or the property of the church."

"What church buys itself custom-finished saloons?"

"Precisely. The ownership becomes of interest."

"Can we check it?"

"Certainly. When we get home I'll phone the A.A." He slowed the engine as we moved through heavy sheets of rain. "The most interesting thing about tonight's encounter, you know, was the fact that that greasy pair didn't take our money. They're mercenary as hell, but they refused an easy hundred rand. Why? As I see it, only two factors would prevent their cashing in. First, they could be scared to talk. And second, they could know they stand to profit more by not talking."

"You mean they've been bribed by the other people on Kate's list."

"More specific than that, by one of the two names we haven't yet established. It must have struck you that Percy's current employer may well be the M.S. or the I.H. on the list? And that would place one of those two in the higher echelons of industry, a man rich enough to pay Kandell's price, and crooked enough to indulge in large-scale industrial spying. On the whole, I'd say that Percy works for Mortimer Silke, and that his message to us reads as follows: 'Neither I, nor any member of my family is implicated in the plan to kill Gretha Corbitt. My boss Mr Silke knows nothing about it, but is anxious to discover what you know. He will pay a good deal more than a hundred rand for the information.' That may all be bluff, of course. It could well be that Silke did hire Bergen, and is afraid you may have evidence against him. Anyway, I'll take you a bet that right now Percy is on the 'phone, making a full report on everything we said tonight."

A goose walked over my grave, and I shivered. Evan nodded gravely. "Yes, Lennie. If these people thought it necessary to kill Gretha, then they may think it necessary to kill us. You must be careful. Don't go anywhere alone, or without telling me. Don't try and be clever. And don't put your trust in Dave Leatherhead."

I said, "I'll probably never see him again."

In fact I saw him the very next morning, at Cory Bergen's funeral.

❦ ❦ ❦

XXVI

I HADN'T THOUGHT they'd bury him so soon. Somehow I imagined that because it was a violent death, they'd keep his body in the morgue for a long time, but Evan said they'd done the post mortem very quickly, there was no doubt that decapitation was the cause of death, and the funeral was being rushed to avoid the sensation-seekers.

Evan said, "I spoke to Sharvey before breakfast. He sounded distraught, poor chap."

"They haven't found Gretha's body?"

"No. They've taken off part of the roof and lifted the staircase. It shouldn't be long now ... but the strain ..."

"What time's the funeral?"

"Nine, at the crematorium."

"Are you going?"

"Yes."

"I'll go with you."

We were at the cemetery by eight-thirty, left the car by the main gate and walked down the road to the gate of the crematorium. It was a gusty day and I had my head down so I didn't see Dave until I was actually in the memorial garden. He stepped out of nowhere and grasped my arm, giving me a dreadful fright.

"Hullo, Lennie." He had on a dark suit and looked older and grimmer than I remembered. His grip on my arm hardened. "I want to talk to you."

"I can't. Not now."

"There's no one here yet except the undertakers and Bergen's cadaver. They won't bother us."

Evan said sharply, "You have some explaining to do, Leatherhead," and Dave looked at him.

"So let me start explaining." He drew us to a bench between two horrid little banks of wreaths and imortelles. I sat down next to him, but Evan remained standing.

"A quick change," Dave said. "A couple of days ago we were friends."

"A couple of days ago," said Evan, "you were caught in a lie."

Dave frowned an enquiry, and Evan met his eye. "On Tuesday morning I called round at Chopping and Spicer's. I asked whether you were employed by them and they said you were not. I told them you had been seen taking pictures on the Peak Hill site and they said they knew nothing about it. As I left the building I saw you arrive in the company of Derek Sharvey. You were chatting like old cronies, although you'd given us to understand you had no acquaintance with anyone in Michael Crescent. So?"

"Who said I worked for Chopping and Spicer?"

139

"You did," I told him. "The first time we met, on Peak Hill, I asked if you worked for them and you said 'indirectly'."

Dave's face cleared. "Ah, I see. I was being sarcastic, my dear. I don't work for them. As a matter of fact, they work for me."

"Oh, now . . ."

"Don't interrupt, Lennie. I'm on the Board of the company responsible for the Peak Hill project. Chopping and Spicer are the agents we employ here. By the rates they charge, you could say we worked for them."

Evan glanced at me. "We can check that."

"You can indeed," said Dave.

"And Sharvey? How is it you were chatting to him?"

This time the answer was slower in coming. "I approached Sharvey and made him an offer for his house."

"It's not his house, it's Nell's."

"I know about that, and also that she's refused many offers by my firm. I thought maybe she'd have changed her mind, since we started work on the site. Sharvey would like to sell, but he told me his wife still won't budge." Dave's mouth curled like a cat's. "Maybe she'll think again, now that half the place is in ruins."

I shivered, and his eyes mocked me. "Scared, Lennie?"

I shook my head and he sighed. "You should be, you know. I wish you'd trust me. No? Well, the only thing I can say is, make those checks. You'll find I'm what I say I am. When you're ready, whistle and I'll come running."

"I don't want to see you again," I said.

He got up at once and started to walk away. I couldn't bear to see him leave like that and I tried to think of some way to stop him that was dignified, but all I could dredge up was a squeaked "Dave!"

He turned round at once, came back and tried to put his arms round me.

"No!" I said, and he let me go. "Tell me one thing," I said, "and I'll know whether you're on my side or not."

"Well?"

"Who is I.H.?"

140

He stared at me, his face went red and he opened his mouth in a sort of exasperation.

"Lennie, if I could answer that, I would."

"You could, but you won't," I said. "It's against orders, isn't it?"

Dave turned away from me and spoke to Evan. "Since you've fired the watchdog, Doc, you'd better start barking yourself. Don't let Lennie out of your sight. When they find Gretha Corbitt, all hell will break loose, and that won't be long now. If anything happens to Lennie in the next twelve hours, it's on your head."

He swung on his heel and ran up the steps to the road. At the gate he nearly bumped into a group of people, Nell and Derek Sharvey with Nick Corbitt between them. Sharvey was busy helping Nick down the steps, and never saw us, but Nell did, and turned aside and came over to where we stood.

⑤ ⑤ ⑤

XXVII

SHE LOOKED LIKE death.

I don't mean the conventional figure of death, although she was dressed in black. It was her face. Something incredibly ancient had touched it. I thought, doom looks like that, and she put her hand on my shoulder.

"You shouldn't be here, Lennie."

As I started to speak she made an impatient gesture. "I warned you to leave this alone. Why did you disobey me?"

141

"I am involved," I said.

"Involved? Guilty, you mean. You put that advertisement in the paper, didn't you?"

"If you'd told me what I wanted to know, I wouldn't have needed to advertise. You knew about Greco and the others. Why did you keep quiet about them?"

"Do you think I had any choice? You're as arrogant as she was. You understand nothing, suffer nothing, yet you don't hesitate to judge. You make idiotic decisions, and innocent people die for them."

"Cory Bergen was no innocent."

"I'm not talking about Cory, I'm talking about Gretha. I hold you responsible for her death. If you'd listened to me she would have been in no danger."

It was so blatantly unfair that I could feel the red come up into my face.

"Haven't you considered, Mrs Sharvey, that Gretha may still be alive?"

Then she said a terrifying thing. She said, "God forbid," and meant it. "If Gretha is dead," she said, "that may be the end of it. If she lives, none of us is safe."

I suppose she saw the look on my face, for she drew a sudden deep breath and closed her eyes. When she opened them again her anger had faded. She said briskly,

"Don't go near my brother, please. He can't stand any more emotional strain. If you must stay here, please sit at the back where he can't see you."

She walked away. I found I was trembling. Beside me, Evan began to mutter under his breath and his hand jogged my elbow. "Come on."

"You're not leaving?"

"Certainly not. These people may crack wide open any minute, and if they do I want to be around. If I cause a little emotional strain," his gnome's face twinkled at me, "well, that's their funeral."

XXVIII

T HE SERVICE SEEMED to be happening in another
world. The kindly priest, speaking of redemption and mercy,
was a figure in a tableau. The reality was with the onlookers. I
watched them. Nick Corbitt sat hunched in the front row, his
eyes on the coffin. Nell was upright beside him, her hands folded
in her lap. Had she sent all the flowers that crowded the
antiseptic tiles of the floor? No one else would mourn Cory
Bergen. There was an officer from his old regiment. Pin neat,
punctilious, far too young to remember the war. A few other
people were behind the Corbitts, neighbours, perhaps, from
Michael Crescent.

Who paid Cory Bergen?

The same that killed Kate Falconer.

Who needed her death?

My own father? He had no reason.

Greco, who desired the Falconer property? The Kandells,
who were Greco's agents?

Johan Dessels, the frustrated lover, or Gretha Corbitt, who
might be more ready to kill Kate than lose her to some unknown
man?

Nick Corbitt, the cold man who could not warm himself at any
woman's fire?

Nell Sharvey or Derek, whose heart was in material possessions?

Morty Silke? The I.H. we did not yet know?

M.S. and I.H. The Pelican and the Eagle.

Of all the birds, the eagle is king.

The king of predators, but no toucher of carrion. The symbol of
courage, independence, of lofty magnificence. The black eagle was
the man Kate loved. I should have realised that at once.

My thoughts were broken by a rumbling sound. The coffin was
rolling back, past the tired-looking velvet curtain, to the profes-
sionals and the funeral fire.

Nick Corbitt had his hands over his face, Nell was bending over

143

him. Derek Sharvey stumbled to his feet and came plunging blindly past us, looking as if he were about to faint. I got up and hurried after him, but he was out in the road before I caught up with him. When I touched his arm, he spun round and gave a cry as if I were something risen from the graveyard.

"It's only me," I said.

He wiped his sleeve over his face.

"You looked . . ."

". . . like Kate?"

"Yes. For a moment. I'm . . . it's that damned service. Dust unto dust. I kept thinking of Gretha. God, I can't stand this any longer."

"Sit down." There was a bus seat and I drew him to it. Thick trees shadowed us. Derek's face shone in the gloom, sweat trickled down his temples.

"She's alive," I said. He gave me a shocked glance.

"What?"

"I feel she's alive."

He began to laugh, almost hysterically. "Oh, now, not another Cassandra, that's Gretha's . . ." He stopped, his eyelids fluttered and he sagged forward, over his knees. After a while he leaned right back again. I got a good look at him. It wasn't grief he felt, it was panic. He was half silly with fright. He said under his breath, "She must be dead by now."

I said nothing, and he turned to scan my face. "Nobody told you anything? They haven't found her?"

"Not to my knowledge. But they will find her, and alive." Deliberately, I kept my voice low, almost whispering. Sharvey watched me, his mouth drooping open.

"You know," he said. "Don't you?" He began to fumble in his pocket, produced a handkerchief and mopped his face. His little black eyes sharpened into focus. "I'll pay you," he said. "If you go away and say nothing, I'll pay what I can."

"It's not me you have to bargain with," I said.

"Who then?"

"M.S." I said. "I.H."

"I don't know them. If I knew, I'd have gone to them long ago. I'm not a fool."

"I.H. the Black Eagle."

"No. It means nothing, nothing."

"And the Pelican? Morty Silke?"

Sharvey blinked. It was plain surprise that crossed his face. "Silke? I remember . . . something. Yes. Silke." He peered at me.

"You're in touch with him?"

"I don't know where to find him."

Sharvey frowned. "I think it was Horne and Culverwell. But that was years ago."

"Johannesburg?"

"Industrial chemicals, something like that. What are you going to do?" There was an eagerness in his voice he couldn't hide and I thought, yes, Mr Sharvey, you hope that I'll find them and they'll do the silencing for you. Standing up, I said, "I think your wife is looking for you."

Nell Sharvey was waiting at the top of the steps. She raised one hand imperiously. Sharvey seemed for a moment to resist the summons, but then he went up the slope to her side. They went back to the chapel, I suppose to collect Nick and talk to the other people there. I sat quietly on the bench until Evan joined me.

$\oint$ $\oint$ $\oint$

XXIX

"How long will it be," I said, "before they've finished clearing the rubble from that house?" We were sitting in Evan's study. The electric heater was on and there was a pot of coffee between us.

"This morning, the Fire Chief said twelve hours at the

most. That means they should find her before eight o'clock tonight."

We'd put in a good two hours' work. We'd established that Morty Silke was Chairman of Horne and Culverwell and a great many other concerns. We knew that the maroon Mercedes in the Kandell's garage was registered with one of these. We'd checked Dave Leatherhead's credentials and found he'd spoken the truth.

I said, "I think you should 'phone Dave."

Evan didn't answer, he just got up and went to the telephone, and dialled a number. After a moment he said, "I'd like to speak to Mr David Leatherhead, please." A pause, and then, "I see. Can you tell me if he left a forwarding address? Yes. Thank you." He wrote on a pad, repeating as he did so, "77 Theunissen Street, Inanda, Johannesburg".

Replacing the receiver, he gave me a stony look. "Your friend has left. Gone to Johannesburg, one jump ahead of us."

I stood up. "Could we get the next 'plane."

Evan glanced at his watch. "Might." He reached for the 'phone again.

By 11.45 we were at the airport, by noon on the Boeing, and by 1.00 p.m. were nosing down towards the sprawl of Jo'burg, city of declining gold, the place where Morty Silke lived, the far place from which came Kate Falconer's death.

XXX

We made a plan during the flight. We would drive straight to the centre of town on the airport 'bus, 'phone Morty Silke and tell him we wanted to see him. We felt sure he'd be expecting us, since Kandell or Dave Leatherhead must have passed the news that we'd identified him.

Like so many plans, it went wildly astray.

To begin with, we were trailed from the airport; not skilfully, but blatantly, by a trio of obvious ex-pugs. They'd have been funny if they hadn't scared me so much.

The first was a huge Cro-Magnon with a broken nose, black shirt, black leather jacket and tan pants. The second was built like a bullfrog and wore an electric yellow shirt and a royal blue suit. They followed us across the concourse. Every time I looked back, there they were, two paces behind with their hands hanging loose. Outside, when we boarded the bus, they climbed into a Buick with a glare-proof windscreen. The driver was a black man. He wore a white sweater with "Charlie's Gym" embroidered in red on the breast.

The Buick followed us all the way into town. I pointed this out to Evan, who grunted and said everyone had to take the same road and I mustn't let my imagination overset my reason.

When we reached town, we 'phoned Silke's office and met with another set-back. He wasn't there, and his secretary refused to say where we could find him. We searched the 'phone book for a home number, but there was none listed. We were feeling pretty foolish when I remembered Ruth Reibstein.

Ruth's father is one of the richest men in Africa. A few years ago she slipped the platinum leash and went to Europe and the States to study art, which is how I met her. She was now back in Jo'burg, running her own gallery. She still moved with the jet set and might know Morty Silke.

147

We took a taxi to the gallery. This time, when the Buick fell in behind us, Evan didn't have any snide remarks to offer.

We found Ruth checking through a stack of canvasses, her hair full of plastic straw. She squawked, kissed me, beamed at Evan, and asked what I was doing on the Rand.

"Looking for a Mr Mortimer Silke."

"Silke?" She pushed her glasses up her forehead and blinked at me. "Some of your best friends are hyenas?"

"Is he that bad?"

"Look, he makes the scene. It's just, nobody likes him. He arrives from the backveld with no seat to his pants and in no time he wants to buy out De Beers. He's a smart promoter. Too smart, too smart to get caught."

"You mean he's crooked."

"I'd say, as a clover crossing."

"Would he go in for industrial spying?"

"Probably."

"Is he married?"

Ruth's thin fingers flicked disparagingly. "I'll say. Half the money, she made. Looks dumb, but she plays bridge for two rand a hundred and shows a steady profit. She's on all the best fund-raising committees. You want to raise a million in a month, you need faith, hope and Hilary."

"Hilary! Was her maiden name Kandell or Kennedy?"

"I wouldn't know, honey."

"Could you arrange for me to meet her?"

"I suppose so. When?"

"This afternoon. Now."

Ruth went away and did some telephoning. When she came back, she grinned at me. "This very afternoon, at the home of Mr and Mrs Morty Silke, is a charity *braaivleis*. Go burn some steak, be my guest." She peered out through the glass door on to the street. "How did you come?"

"Taxi."

"You better take my car. It's way beyond Bryanston where the Silkes live."

Her car, which stood in a cul de sac beside the shop, was a Thunderbird. Evan took one look at it and climbed into the driver's seat. When I tried to argue he said, "You don't know Johannesburg, I do." He was right. I thanked Ruth, told her we'd return the car before nightfall, got in and started praying. Not that Evan is a bad driver. He can make a car do anything, that's the trouble. It wasn't till we cleared the city centre that I dared lift my head from the rally-seat. The Buick was right on our tail. Evan glanced in the mirror and said happily, "I'll lose them, don't worry."

Halfway along the main trunk road, he made his bid. He took the Thunderbird up to sixty, shifting it through the traffic easily enough. Behind us the cumbersome Buick lurched crazily. Blackjacket, who was driving, seemed to be cursing all the time. Bullfrog had his eyes shut. After seven minutes by my sweat-misted watch, they were still with us. Then we got a break. The traffic thickened and closed behind a huge cement-mixer that was making an effort to turn left down a side street. Evan, with a burst of speed, overtook the mixer, swung round it under the nose of the cab, lurched into the gutter, skidded out again, and shot along the side road. I caught one glimpse of the driver, crouched over his wheel and pounding after us at his full forty m.p.h. Then we were out on a tertiary road, and more or less alone.

I didn't try to follow our direction from there on. At ten minutes past four we drove through the gates of the Silke home.

It was stockbroker's Taj Mahal. Its towers and domes hung above distant trees like a bulbous nose above a tankard. Immediately on our left was a paddock filled with Jags and Mercedes and the occasional Porsche. Evan nosed the Thunderbird in among them and we climbed out.

Straight ahead a driveway headed for the mansion. On the right of the drive was a large shrubbery, almost a wood. I heard a willow-warbler in there, and saw a scrub-robin jerking his tail on a high branch.

Beyond the shrubbery was the garden proper, terraced lawns and borders. The nearest level was evidently where the *braai* was going to happen, because there were several pits already glowing with coals, and big stalls with white tablecloths where

149

men in white jackets were laying out packets of raw meat, bread and salads. There was a bar under a group of trees. A couple of hundred people were milling about close to the bar area. Nobody took any notice of Evan and me. I asked a bar attendant where Mrs Silke was, and he said he wasn't sure, maybe she was up at the house. Evidently Hilary didn't believe in the personal appearance bit.

We scaled three terraces, walked round an Olympic-size pool, and reached the front door. Here I stopped.

"Evan, I want to go in alone." As he started to argue, I said, "there's a much better chance she'll talk to me without a witness. If I'm not back in thirty minutes, you call the police, and if anything blows up out here, you come in for me."

He didn't like it, but he saw it made sense, so he went back to the top of the first terrace, and I pressed the door-bell.

It was opened by a long-nosed Zanzibari who looked as if he played Acol. He told me Mrs Silke was not available, and I asked him to take in my name, and he shook his head, and I got a foot in the door, and at that point a woman appeared in the hall and asked what the noise was about.

I ducked my head past the Zanzibari and called, "Mrs Silke? My name is Leonora Bryant. I have to speak to you, please."

She came slowly forward, a fat sleek woman with brown hair done up in high puffs and scrolls. She nodded to the henchman, who stepped aside. I was in.

Mrs Hilary Silke was living proof that bell-bottomed women shouldn't wear bell-bottomed trousers. Her black cat-suit strained across her buttocks and her short thick thighs. She had the bright Kandell eyes in a heavy, rubbery face. Tangerine lipstick emphasised the ugliness of a mouth overfilled with small, sharp, shining teeth. She had small hands covered with rings and small feet laced into cork-soled sandals. In one hand she carried a transistor radio. It tinkled inanely between us as she looked me over.

"You better come in here," she said at last.

I followed her across the hall, through a huge door studded with silver nails, and into a sort of seraglio. It was a big room, marble-floored, with a couple of beautiful Persian carpets and some horribly phoney Persian pottery. The walls on the left and right were little more than stone screens, pierced with an intricate design of flowers and fruit. At the far end there was no wall, but a huge glassed aviary. Trees grew in it, and their branches were full of tropical birds, parakeets and parrots and cockatiels and at least two birds of paradise. The din they made was fantastic. The light in the room was greenish, and the air warm and humid. I guessed it was specially moisturised.

In the centre of the floor was a circle of low couches covered in leather. In the middle of the circle, an African Grey swung upside down from a gilt perch. As we approached, he fingered himself upright and started pitching sunflower-seed all over the floor. His bald red eye mocked me.

Hilary Silke waved me to one of the sofas and sprawled back on another herself. Her tongue poked about in her mouth as she watched me. After a while she helped the tongue along with a little finger. She said, "Why did you come here, Miss Bryant?"

If she wanted it rude she could have it rude. I said, "Not to burns *boerewors*, Mrs Silke."

"So?"

"I'm here to talk about Kate Falconer, my aunt who died. You knew her when you were Miss Kandell, in Durban."

The sage-green eyes never left me. "Who said so?"

"I have proof."

"Who sent you here?"

"No one."

"How do you know my name?"

"I was told it." I paused deliberately. "I met your father this week."

"How?"

"He answered an advertisement I placed in the newspaper, concerning the Kolumbe Wild Life Quiz. He won first prize. I felt sure he'd told you all about it."

Her mouth twisted. "Percy never entered a quiz in his life. He doesn't know anything about wild life."

"And yet he visited Kolumbe, in the old days."

Her head jerked sideways. "Who said so?"

"Why, he did. He repaired the roof there, in my grand-father's day. Invented a new sort of tile. He remembered it quite clearly."

Hilary shrugged. "That could be."

"He seems prosperous, your father," I said. "But of course he has your husband's money behind him."

"What d'you mean?"

"I assume your father gets a lot of help from your husband. For instance, his Mercedes is registered to one of Mr Silke's companies. That must be quite a saving."

Hilary nibbled round a thumbnail. "Listen. I don't need you spying round my father."

"Perhaps not. Personally, I find it poetic justice."

She closed her thick lids in simulated long-suffering. "Either tell me what you're after, or go away. I'm busy."

"Very well. In a nut-shell, Mrs Silke, I'm here to ask some questions about the murder of Kate Falconer."

Hilary's mouth opened to expose a tongue as thick and dirty as the parrot's. For a moment no sound came out, and then she managed something like a laugh.

"Don't be such a fool. Your aunt fell out of a boat and got drowned."

"No. Someone killed her."

"Look, you're not selling that crap to me. You weren't around when Kate Falconer died. I was. She drowned."

"You mean you witnessed the event?"

"No, of course not. But I read the papers. I heard what the courts said, they said she took the boat out and it capsized and she fell in the river."

"Strange, though, that her body was never found."

"Sharks. The sharks got it."

"Then you don't think it possible Kate ran away with Greco?"

At the mention of that name, Hilary's face showed sharp dislike, and some fear.

"That one, he'd no chance, and no inclination either."

"Kate found him out in time, didn't she? Found out he

was trying to buy the property cheap from my father, and make a handsome profit?"

She sat absolutely still. I leaned towards her. "You met Greco during the war, in Switzerland. Afterwards, when he bolted for Africa, and you came home, he got in touch with you. You, your father and his sister Lola, your husband-to-be Mortimer Silke, and Greco, got together and fudged up a plan, didn't you? Small in comparison with the money you make now, but at that time you were all beginners. Greco wanted sterling, Mortimer and you and the rest wanted a toe in the property market. Your father knew my father, and Derek Sharvey. That gave him the in. My father was in money difficulties, a soft touch. He wanted to sell, he had to sell, and you put the pinch on him. But Kate found out, didn't she, and there was hell to pay? Because it was her old home that was to be carved up, and turned into a commercial deal.

"Being Kate, she decided to teach you all a lesson. She invited you to a party to be held on October 31st, Hallowe'en. At that party, she intended to show Ralph what a lousy bargain he was getting. No doubt she'd discovered certain facts about your characters; such as that Greco was wanted right across Europe for black marketeering? Perhaps she knew your father was selling Probyn's trade secrets? Anyway, it didn't look as if you were going to enjoy the Hallowe'en party. It became necessary to prevent Kate from holding it. She conveniently disappeared, and when the shouting died down, my father sold the Michael Crescent property, just as you'd planned, and you were all free to enjoy the profits."

It was at this point that I saw I'd lost Hilary's attention. There'd been real fear in her bulbous stare when I started my spiel, but that had gone. She was smiling at the screen wall behind me, and the parrot was looking that way, too, and bobbing up and down along his perch.

Someone in the next room was listening, and it was easy enough to guess who. I turned my head and said, "Why not join us, Mr Silke?"

153

A faint chuckle sounded, and the next minute heels clacked on the marble and round through the archway waddled Kate's Pelican.

Mortimer Silke was very short, with a wide white shirt-front, bandy legs, big splayed feet. Yet somehow, when I looked at him, I thought not of any bird, but of the hollow pumpkins of a Witches' Sabbath. His eyes, set extraordinarily far apart, were so empty of light that they looked like holes with darkness behind them.

"Miss Bryant," he bowed and giggled before me, "I'm so glad to meet you. You're a cheeky girl, but sharp, I'll give you that. Your advertisement!" He moved over to sit on the sofa next to his wife. "Had poor old Percy on the flap, I can tell you. 'Phoning me at all hours, goodness, you'd have thought the world was coming to an end just because you found out we knew your aunt Kate. 'Nothing wrong in that,' I told him, and no more there is. But you shouldn't go round talking of murder, Miss Bryant. That could land you in serious trouble. If I was like some people, I'd be on to my lawyers instead of sitting here chatting to you."

"Did you have me followed from the airport?" I demanded, and the cavernous eyes became even blanker.

"Followed? Certainly not! Who followed you?"

"Three men in a Buick, but we shook them off."

"Clever girl!" I could see him assessing that "we", wondering how many people I'd brought with me and where they were now. He said suddenly, "I never made a penny out of your Dad, you know. Not one penny. I'd like to put your mind at rest about that."

"Thank you."

"No, it's the truth, I want to put you straight." He rolled his big head sideways. "What makes you say she was murdered?"

"How do you think she died?"

"Suicide." The answer came promptly. "I always thought suicide. She acted very depressed and strange the last few days of her life, you know. Manic-depressive type. Must have got herself pregnant, something like that. Of course I didn't say anything like that at the time. What good does it do, and there's the bereaved to think of? But you say 'murdered'. Why?"

154

"Gretha Corbitt told me something."

"About Kate? What did she say?"

"That she saw Kate's body, and not in the river."

There was an intense silence in the room. Even the birds in the aviary had stopped their twittering, and I saw that the sun was almost gone. Morty Silke's face had a coppery hue.

"That's very strange." He frowned at me as if he could somehow suck the truth out of me. "When did she tell you this?"

"Last Saturday."

"And there were others there, too?"

"No. We were alone."

He put his head on one side. "What a pity. No witness. And a mad lady. I'm afraid no one will believe it."

"Someone did."

"Now, who was that?"

"Whoever sent Cory Bergen into her house to kill her."

He nodded gently. "You could say that, but then there's the police who say Bergen went in to help Miss Corbitt against an intruder. With both of them dead, it'd be hard to prove your story, Miss Bryant."

At that moment, the transistor radio in Hilary's lap gave out the signal for the five-thirty news flash. Both Silkes bent their heads over the set to listen. I hesitated, then decided I wasn't going to get anything new out of them. I picked up my purse and started for the door.

Halfway there, though, I heard the word "Corbitt", and stopped. "Police and firemen," said the voice, "continued through last night and today their search of the residence of Miss Gretha Corbitt, the elderly Durban recluse who was feared dead in a bizarre fall of debris. The body of family friend Mr Cory Bergen was recovered on Wednesday, but although the basement levels have now been cleared, no trace of Miss Corbitt or the white Alsatian which was her constant companion, has been found. It is assumed that neither she nor the dog was at home when the accident occurred. Anyone who may have knowledge of their whereabouts is asked to . . ."

I didn't wait to hear the rest. I hurtled across the hall and out into the garden, almost falling over Evan.

155

"Gretha!" I said. "She's alive! She wasn't there!" He gaped at me, and in the house I heard Morty Silke shouting. "Run," I said.

We plunged together down the terraces, past the barbecue pits, through the fringe of the crowd, out on to the drive; and saw, slap in the entrance to the car park, the patient bovine hulks of Bullfrog and Blackjacket. At the same moment they saw us.

We doubled back across the lawn. Out of the tail of my eye I saw Morty Silke, the Zanzibari houseman, and three white-coated attendants, heading down from the house.

"The shrubbery," said Evan, "quick," and darted into the bushes.

The path through the shrubbery swerved and forked, dipped and rose. Evan was going like a four-minute miler, I concentrated on not breaking an ankle. At the third blind rise the two of us ran headlong into a black man. He had on white overalls with "Charlie's Gym" in red on the breast. I shrieked.

"Woman who talks to birds," he said in Zulu, "you'll have to trust me."

I nodded. He took my arm and drew me along a side path, Evan following. Behind us, the hunt yowled, ahead the bushes gave way to a tremendous hedge of clipped privet. The Zulu pushed us through a gap. We emerged in a vegetable garden, neat blocks of green with raspberry canes and marrow-frames and a potting-shed at the far end. Away to the left was the Silke Mahal. Silke, the Zanzibari and the three henchmen were just stepping past the far end of the hedge. They came for us.

The Zulu grunted and then smiled at me. "Go past the shed there, Princess. There's a gate into the road. You too, friend."

But Evan wasn't listening. He was dancing about on his toes, swinging both fists. The Zanzibari reached him and caught hold of his shoulder. I found a hoe and picked it up. Bullfrog and Blackjacket appeared suddenly at our rear and the Zulu stepped past Evan and with a lovely nonchalance knocked the Zanzibari backwards into a stand of runner beans.

After that, things grew confused. The three henchmen with Silke tried to rush the Zulu, who picked up the two nearest and clashed them together like cymbals. The third turned and flung himself blindly back through the fence. Morty Silke aimed a blow at Evan and Evan punched him in the belly. Silke started to pull a gun from under his arm, I ran forward and tripped over my hoe, and Blackjacket reached out an enormous hand and squeezed Morty's wrist. When I picked myself up, Silke was lying in the middle of a manure heap, yelling his head off, and the Zanzibari was sprinting for the house with elbows squared.

Blackjacket dropped the gun into his pocket and said, almost regretfully, "I think it's time to leave. Gimme the key to the Thunderbird, lady, and I'll see it gets home."

I gave him the key, being in no shape to argue. He loped back towards the hedge. Bullfrog and the Zulu, Evan and I, made for the gate.

The big Buick was parked at the kerb, with a man at the wheel. Bullfrog signed to me to get in, and I obeyed. Whoever these people were, they had weight on their side. Also, any enemy of Morty Silke was a friend of mine. I slid into the front seat, Evan after me, and found myself pressed against the shoulder of David Leatherhead.

I said, "What the hell are you doing here?"

He made no answer, but turned his head to make sure the other two men were in the car and then flicked the ignition. The Buick slid from the kerb, made a tight U turn and headed for the main road.

"Leatherhead!" For a man with a swelling lip Evan looked very dignified. "Will you kindly inform us where we are going?"

Dave smiled at him. "Home to dinner." He clearly didn't intend to say more.

I leaned my head back and closed my eyes. I wanted to ask myself questions about the Silkes—like, "What was Hilary afraid of?" She'd been scared all right, until . . . when? Until I spoke about Michael Crescent? So was I right off the beam there? Morty Silke had made his appearance about that time. Was it simply me she feared, did she think I was some criminal lunatic out to attack her?

I thought that over carefully before I discarded it. Morty didn't think I was insane. He believed every word I'd said to him. He knew I'd spoken to Gretha. As long as he thought she was dead, I didn't worry him much, but directly he heard she was still alive, and might corroborate my story, he reacted violently.

It was interesting.

I wasn't altogether disappointed with the afternoon's work.

By six-thirty we were in Hillbrow.

The welfare workers have plenty to say about Hillbrow. They say it has one of the highest density populations in the western world, that it's poor in oxygen and rich in robbers, that it's a hideaway for upper-crust abortionists, pot and heroin addicts, glue-sniffers, tax-dodgers, and queers. On New Year's Eve the Hillbrow revels easily turn to car-bouncing and punch-ups.

That doesn't stop thousands of respectable people from living in the area. The apartment blocks stand as tall as Jack's Beanstalk, and at night the windows glow and the doorways glitter and a million golden spiders of music weave and spin among the roots.

That evening the Friday crowds were already racketing along the pavements. Dave ran the Buick between two leaping neon pillars, along a passageway and into a little parking-ground marked, "Private, Members Only."

I climbed out and looked about me.

We were at the foot of a well. On all four sides the cement walls towered, their feet in the trashcans and their heads in the stars. In one wall was a big circular door made to represent the bottom of a bottle. Standing before this was a fair-headed man in karate kit. He bowed politely to Dave and stepped back into the shadows. The green glass door swung open and we walked through.

℘ ℘ ℘

XXXI

T HERE WAS A door on our right, dark green with the words "Hippo Club" in gilt script. We passed that, and headed for a bank of elevators, Dave leading, Evan and me next, and the two musclemen padding behind. The lift took us softly up to the nineteenth floor. We stepped out into a large hall with rough white walls, a redwood floor, a single abstract painting, several doors.

Dave turned to me. His expression was withdrawn, almost impersonal. He said, "There's plenty of time, Lennie, you'll find all you need through here," and held a door for me as formally as a butler. I heard Evan protest, but I went through the door and closed it after me. I wanted to be quiet a while. My brain seemed to be floating six inches above my skull.

The room was a guest room. In the bathroom leading off it I found big yellow towels and jasmine soap. I stripped and took a quick shower, put on a new face and brushed the mud off my skirt. When I was ready I went out into the hall again.

It was curiously silent. The bodyguards had disappeared. There was no sound of voices. Only the door at the far end of the hall stood open, so I walked through that.

An eyrie, it was. The ceiling was domed, and half of it was glass, with the galaxy white above it. I stood there, unable to tear my eyes from the sight, until a voice said "Over here, Lennie," and I remembered to look round.

Behind me a crescent of chairs was drawn round the hoop of a modern hearth. Dave stood there, a bottle of vodka in one hand, a glass in the other. Next to him, washed, brushed and wearing a dazed look, was Evan. Beyond them, seated in a high-winged chair, her white prophetic face lifted in regal calm, was Gretha Corbitt. At her feet lay the dog Lorca.

⅌ ⅌ ⅌

XXXII

I RAN ACROSS to her, wanting to put my arms round her, I was so glad to see her alive and well; but when I came close to her, I stopped. In some parts of the world they believed the insane are holy. Gretha wasn't far from that inspired madness. I don't know what made her impossible to approach, knowledge, or suffering, or the way her eyes looked straight through and beyond me.

I bent and touched the Alsatian's head. He thumped his tail, but didn't move from his place. Evan said quietly, "How long has she been here?"

"Since Wednesday." Dave watched Gretha's face, but she gave no sign of having heard. "Sit down, both of you, eat and drink and I'll explain."

He gave me a glass of wine and a plate of food that I ate without tasting. He settled himself on the wide plinth beside the hearth, his elbows on his knees, and seemed for a while to gather his thoughts.

At last he raised his head and looked at me. "I've not lied to you, Lennie, but I haven't given you the whole truth. It wasn't possible or wise to do that. It's true that I'm the step-son of Jean-Charles Greco. It's also true that I'm a director of Hamilton Developments. My mother's maiden name was Hamilton, Esther Hamilton, and her shares in the company passed to me when she died four years ago. So I had a perfect right to be on the Peak Hill site, taking photos. But of course, I was there for a special reason. I wanted to study the lay-out of Gretha Corbitt's home.

"A fortnight ago, when the first article appeared in the *Chronicle* about Michael Crescent, I was given instructions by the Chairman of the Board to go to Durban and try to find out its source. I spoke to Derek Sharvey. He lived in the Crescent, knew all the residents. He refused to discuss the article. Then I made him a very good offer for the house. He said it wasn't his to sell, it belonged to his wife, and ... well ... he was obviously very touchy on the subject. I talked him along, and after a while he let slip that he held Gretha Corbitt responsible for the article. Called her 'that screwy sister-in-law of mine'. Then he realised he'd opened his mouth too wide and ended the conversation.

"I realised that the only way I'd get the truth was by talking to Gretha herself. I also realised I wasn't going to get in through the front door. I took a walk around Peak Hill, trying to see if there was any other way in. My pics showed there was, through the hatch in the back wall that Gretha used for groceries. They also showed me that the lower floors of the apartment were out of commission, the windows blocked up. A little talk with the servants in the Crescent, and I knew that Gretha had built herself a miniature fortress in there, and never came out.

"The way things were, I didn't hope too much for a meeting. If I hadn't bumped into you, Lennie, up on the hill, I'd have left Durban that night, most likely. But I did bump into you, and found out you were a Falconer. I thought maybe if you were nosing after the facts, you'd be better placed to get to them, and my best chance was to stay close to you. Which I did. Sure enough, in a few days you came up with the story of the Hallowe'en party, and you had the favours Gretha gave you to prove it. You'd spoken to the Corbitts and Sharvey and you were all set to trace Johan Dessels.

"Up to that point, you were still within the safety limit; what took you past it was that advertisement. That put both you and Gretha in extreme danger. You see, the advert must have made it clear to the people concerned in the party, that the first article was no fluke, but a deliberate attempt to call attention to Kate Falconer's death. I felt sure most of them would attribute the advert to Gretha herself. They might be anxious to forget the past, but Gretha had always shown signs of wanting to recall it. It seemed to me one of them might easily decide to silence Gretha, and you too, since you seemed to be in touch with her.

"Unfortunately, you didn't make it easy for me to talk straight to you. You didn't trust me. You wouldn't listen to me, or to Evan, when we told you to take care. Even Nell Sharvey didn't seem able to scare you off. Indeed I was landed with one woman who was pretty defenceless, and another who had no sense of self-preservation. I couldn't watch you both. It became necessary to get one of you out of the danger zone. The obvious one was Gretha."

"You mean," I said, "you just decided to kidnap her?"

Dave gave me a quizzical look. "No love. We're not all as unprincipled as you. I decided to try and talk to Gretha.

"On Tuesday afternoon, I bought a crate of minerals from the supermarket and put it into her grocery hatch. I left a note tucked among the bottles. The note said I was a friend of yours, that you believed she was in grave danger, that I was utterly trustworthy, and that I would call for her at eight o'clock that night.

"I was back at the hatch right on time. The crate was gone and the inner gate was unlocked. I slithered through, feeling like something out of Peter Pan. Gretha was waiting for me on the other side, with a gun.

Dave picked up his vodka glass and took a long pull at it. "The next ten minutes," he said, "were grotty. Gretha asked me a great many questions. I answered them truthfully, but the answers didn't seem to please her much. All the time the gun was pointing at my navel and Lorca's nose was running up and down my trouser-leg. Finally Gretha stopped asking questions and said,

" 'He was here tonight.'

" 'Who,' I said, 'Bergen?' and she nodded.

" 'He came along the hedge. Lorca heard him and warned me. I shouted and he went away.'

"I said, 'He might kill you, you know, if you don't come with me'.

"It was a wild shot, but it seemed to find the mark. She stood there in the moonlight, chewing her lip and looking at me, and then she suddenly said, 'We'll come.'

"That's all there was to it, except for one thing. Before we left she made me walk round the house with her. She unlocked the front door and left it so. She made me break the latch on one of the back windows. She said, 'If he wants to get in, he can, now'."

Dave stopped speaking and glanced at Gretha. She was bending forward to caress Lorca's head. Our conversation appeared not to interest her.

"I sent her up here on one of the company's light aircraft," said Dave. "The rest you know."

"Not quite." Evan spoke for the first time. "For instance, we don't know why Hamilton Developments should take such an interest in Michael Crescent that a director of the firm must go to Durban to check up on a newspaper feature. Unless the man who sent you also happens to be I.H.?"

Somewhere behind us there was a movement. As I swung round, a man rose from a chair near the door and advanced down the room. Gretha Corbitt got swiftly to her feet and hurried to meet him. He put out an arm and gave her a gentle hug and then looked past her at us.

"You're quite right, Dr Cruickshank. My name is Ivo Hamilton. David is a director of my firm but he's also my nephew, and it was on my private instructions that he went to Durban."

⑨ ⑨ ⑨

XXXIII

IVO HAMILTON WAS big, tough and elegant. He must have stood about six-three or -four, but bone and muscle were so well balanced that he didn't seem clumsy. His eyes, light brown with very dark pupils, had a wary look, as if he spent a lot of time close to dangerous events or people. His dark hair was thick and rather wiry, but short, and his skin too was dark, with colour on the cheekbones. His nose was strong, his mouth long and patient and unsmiling. But what made you look at him was the feeling that behind the patience was a physical power that might be explosive, and a mental force that might not accept normal standards. He wore dark slacks, a dark red smoking jacket, a fine lawn shirt. His cufflinks looked like onyx.

He could be a tycoon or a racketeer, but he couldn't belong anywhere else than in the world of affairs. There wasn't anything professional or academic about him. Also he was very much at home. It was clear the minute he stood up that this apartment belonged to him, and that he expected everyone in it to do what he told them without argument.

Evan said, "You've acted in a pretty arrogant manner, Mr Hamilton."

A look of faint surprise touched Hamilton's face. "Have I? You mean the boys? I'm sorry. I suppose you've had a pretty torrid afternoon. You left Durban so fast I couldn't fix it any other way." He glanced at me. "If I'd sent Dave to the airport to meet you, would you have accepted his directions?"

"Probably not," I admitted.

"That's what I thought. Another thing, Dave would never have got past the Silkes' gate. Too many people know him. It was necessary to give you some sort of protection. As a rule Morty's a grass-snake, but he can be venomous in a crisis."

"In which case," said Evan furiously, "why did you allow Lennie to meet him at all? You appear to be omniscient, you evidently knew quite well we were headed for the Silkes', because your men got there even after I'd lost them. Why didn't you come out to the airport, identify yourself in a civilised manner, and you and I could have made some plan to interview Silke ourselves?"

"That wouldn't have been any good, you know. Neither of us could have frightened Morty in the least. It had to be Lennie. Besides, she wanted to go."

"And since when have you concerned yourself in Lennie's affairs?"

The light eyes regarded Evan thoughtfully. "About the same length of time as you have, Doctor. I must admit, my concern became greater a fortnight ago, when that first thing appeared in the *Chronicle*. Since then, I've had Lennie watched constantly."

"Watched!?" I said. "By whom?"

"Oh, Dave, and others. I've a lot of contacts." He didn't seem to think the matter of much importance, and his arrogance infuriated me.

"Let me tell you, Mr Hamilton, I don't need your protection. I have Evan to look after me. He's been wonderful to me always."

"Yes, he has." Hamilton's smile was genuine and attractive. "But Dr Cruickshank knows nothing of violence."

"And you do, I take it?"

"Yes." He glanced at Gretha, who all this time had remained standing close to him, her sombre gaze fixed on his face. He led her gently to the wing chair, lifted the glass of wine she had left untouched, and placed it in her hands. She took a few sips from it, and then leaned back in the chair with closed eyes. Ivo Hamilton came and sat beside me on the sofa. "Violence in the war," he said, "and afterwards. It's not all physical, you know, and plenty of it is quite legitimate. I promoted fights for some time. The Hippo Club downstairs belongs to me. A lot of the ring men use it."

"Men like Cory Bergen?"

"No. Bergen was out long before my time. He used to go berserk. He was dropped. I never met him."

"And now you're one hundred per cent respectable? Hamilton Developments, nine to five?"

"I always had that. My father left it to my sister Esther and me. Mink-lined play-pen." All the time he spoke, he was studying me with an absorbed expression. Suddenly he smiled and I found myself smiling back. I had to remind myself that Ivo Hamilton was not only arrogant, but might easily be a murderer. I tried to break the spell he seemed to weave so easily.

"Then Jean-Charles Greco was your brother-in-law?"

"For a while. His marriages are kind of seasonal. He thought Esther would bring him money, but it was well tied up. Still, she did leave her husband for him, and marry him, and stick with him for ten years."

"I'm surprised you allowed it."

He took that seriously. "No way of stopping it. She was crazy about him. Her husband was a nothing, anyway. When she divorced Greco, I brought her and Dave back home. She died four years ago, and Dave inherited her share."

I shook my head. "Hamilton Developments," I said, "and all the time we were trying to trace I.H. that damn board was on Peak Hill, staring us in the face. Did you buy the site because of Kate?"

A stillness came to his face, a sharpening of the eyes and mouth that made him formidable. Then he shrugged. "Perhaps. It didn't mean much to her. Not Michael Crescent. It was the shack she loved."

"Yes, that's what Johan Dessels said."

"She wasn't a townswoman."

I wanted to go on asking him about Kate, but I didn't dare. He'd retreated again, to that patience of his. Then, just when it seemed the silence could never be broken, he spoke again, heavily. "I suppose we have to talk about her."

He leaned forward, picked up the wine-bottle and topped up my glass. As his wrist brushed my hand, I felt the high tension tremor in his flesh. He turned the bottle and looked at it and then set it gently on the floor at his feet.

"Kate was good," he said. "You must believe that, whatever the rest say. Not a do-gooder, not always moral. She did some crazy things, slept around a bit, Evan will have told you, but she was good. She gave out something people needed. A sort of ... vivid compassion. It drew people to her, the good and the bad. She was water in a dry place.

"I met her by chance. Only knew her for three months. It was the one good thing that came out of the war, for me. There was a military reunion down in Durban. Someone dragged me to it. Nick Corbitt was there. There was a party and we all got pretty high. Corbitt invited us for a final round at his house, and Kate was there, with Nell and some others.

Eleven hours after I met her, I decided I was going to marry her."

"Did she love you?" Suddenly I wanted to know that, very much.

He shook his head. "I don't know."

"Nell Sharvey told me she did. She said that in the last weeks of Kate's life, it was obvious she was in love."

He turned his head to look at me. "She loved me, but I don't know if she loved me enough. There was never time to be sure. She never said she'd marry me. I was important to her, she was happy with me, but she closed off part of her life from me. I never met her friends. I thought at the time it was because my own circle was questionable, but later, I realised there was someone between us all the time."

"Who?"

He gave a crooked smile. "You."

"Me?" I stared at him and he said, "She looked after you for a year, you know. She was devoted to you. Sometimes when I spoke about marriage, she'd frown and say, 'I don't know, Ivo, I have to think of the child,' and it's plain she meant, 'my child'."

I thought about that. "Yes, she said the same thing to Dessels. He misunderstood. He thought she was pregnant."

"No. Kate meant you. She loved you, she loved her work, she loved Kolumbe, and she loved me, but you came first. What got me was that I didn't take up the whole of her life. I was jealous as hell. I wanted to be supreme, I wanted to shut out everything and everyone but myself. That's why she died."

Gretha Corbitt stirred in her chair and moaned. The man beside me didn't seem to hear her. Sweat shone on his face and on the backs of his hands.

"It was October 25th. I'd been down in Durban for a week. The days passed and I couldn't get her to say she'd marry me. Sometimes she came very close to saying it. Then she'd retract. It . . . it just sent me mad. I was young, I hadn't learned to control my temper. That night, I blew up. I asked her what kind of bitch she was, to sleep with me and then turn me down as if that's all I was good for. I tried to bully her into giving an answer. It was a fool thing to do. She was worried stiff at the time, about your father. He'd run into debt, got on the wrong side of Sharvey, and Kate was trying to keep things on an even keel. The things I said to her sent her into a rage, and she yelled at me and I yelled back and eventually I stormed out and flew back to the Rand. I cooled off fast enough. If I'd had any sense I'd have telephoned or written straight away, but I tried to be clever. I decided to give her time to miss me. I had it all worked out. I'd leave her alone until after the week-end, and on Tuesday I'd go down and stage the big reconciliation. But at mid-day on Monday the news came over the radio. She was missing.

"I got down to Durban as fast as I could. By the time I reached Kolumbe, they'd found her dinghy. They were looking for her body. I joined one of the search parties. But it was no good. There was no trace.

"I stayed in town for three days. The arguments started, about where Kate was. There was the rumour she'd run off with someone. I knew that wasn't true, and I knew she never committed suicide. I believed it was an accident, and I blamed myself for that. She'd gone out to Kolumbe to sort things out in her mind, taken the boat out and capsized it. If I'd been near, she might have talked to me instead. That's how it seemed to me, and I thought perhaps I should go to the police and talk to them; but I decided against that. It would give the press another story, and the gossips a little more dirt to throw at Kate. It wouldn't help. She was dead. There was nothing else in the world that mattered."

Again Gretha moaned. I looked at her. She was swaying back and forth, her outstretched hands gripping the arms of her chair, her wide-open eyes fixed on Ivo Hamilton. From her throat came the crooning that a primitive woman makes to ease physical pain. "Ai! Ai!"

"Gretha." I rose and put a hand on her shoulder. She shifted her gaze to me.

"Dead," she said. "Kate's dead. Where shall I go to now?" Ivo Hamilton came quickly past me and knelt at her side.

"Gretha? You saw Kate, didn't you?"

"Dead . . ." the word trailed and Ivo caught it up.

"Dead. You saw her? Lying somewhere, on the floor, was it?"

168

"On the couch. So strange. She breathed so lightly, and her eyes were so dark. She looked like a cat in the dusk. She stared at me but she never saw me. Then he shut the door. But I hid. I waited and I saw him carry her..."

"Who did you see?" Ivo spoke in a whisper, but it woke Gretha. The rocking of her body stopped. She frowned at him with a troubled air, and then smiled.

"It wasn't you. You're kind to me. You brought me to this nice place. There's no river here. Did he put her in the river?"

Terror sprang across her face, and Ivo said gently. "No. Forget about the river. Look at the sky instead." She tilted her face obediently upwards. Ivo watched her for a moment, then slowly got to his feet.

"It's gone. Several times, she's nearly spoken, but she shies away." He glanced from Evan to me, and for the first time that evening, looked discomforted. "You do see the implication of what she has said?"

"Yes," said Evan. "That Kate died at Kolumbe shack, and there were other people with her when she died. Gretha, and at least one other of the Corbitt family, since she could not have gone unaccompanied. Bergen, probably, too. Nick couldn't have lifted a body, let alone have carried it any distance. My God, when I think how they fooled us! They must have got her out there on some pretence..."

"No." Ivo spoke deliberately. "They went to the shack on Kate's invitation, and they went on October 31st. That Hallowe'en party was never cancelled."

"But..." I struggled to pull my thoughts together... "they all confirmed it was cancelled. Not just the Corbitts, everyone. My father testified in court..."

"Yes, he did. I'm sure he spoke the truth. I'm sure Kate told him the party was off, and I'm equally convinced she let the rest come. Remember, Lennie, I was one of those invited. I received no word of cancellation."

"But you'd quarrelled with Kate, you were away in Johannesburg."

"She knew where to get hold of me if she wanted. She didn't

choose to do so. She expected me to attend. If I'd got there, instead of indulging my vanity, Kate wouldn't have died."

"What evidence have you got to support such a theory?" asked Evan.

Ivo didn't answer directly. His eyes rested on the woman in the wing chair. "Do you remember where Gretha collected those Hallowe'en favours?"

Evan shook his head, and I said, "She told me, 'From the table'."

"Exactly. From the supper table at the shack, where they had been set out to mark the guests' places."

It was true. Each of us knew that. Evan spoke first. "You'll never prove any of this."

"I might."

"How?" I said.

Ivo raised his head and looked at me. "By frightening them. A direct confrontation."

"You mean, at the shack?"

"Something like that." He was watching me with an intent, almost measuring expression. Evan stepped forward.

"You'll not take Lennie there. I won't have it."

"Please Evan," I began, and he caught hold of my shoulder and turned me to face him.

"Listen to me," he said. "Hasn't it occurred to you that you could be walking straight into a trap? This man is a stranger to you. What if he was also at that party? He could be as guilty as any of them. Why should you trust him?"

"Gretha trusts him," I said. "She wouldn't, if he'd been at the shack that night."

"Gretha! What weight can you give her fancies? In practical terms, they're worthless."

"Then everything else we've learned through her is worthless."

"For the love of God," his hands gripped my shoulders, "let it go. It's enough, now. Two people have died. Your father decided to hold his peace, do the same Lennie, do the same."

I looked at the others in the room. Ivo Hamilton stood a little apart, brooding, his big shoulders hunched as if he wanted no part in my decision. Dave looked anxious and unhappy. Only Gretha seemed unaware of any strain. She lifted her face towards the stars like a child without care. I wondered what was going to happen to her. If we recreated the past, mightn't that push her into total madness? Yet if we did nothing, how did that help her? Sooner or later she must come out of hiding, and be sent home. And then? She still held her knowledge of Kate's death. How long would she survive, while the killer ran free?

Turning back, I met Evan's gaze, full of love, and fear, and warning. I didn't say anything, but after a moment he stepped away from me, spreading his hands in resignation.

"Very well." He spoke to Ivo. "We accept; but on certain conditions."

"Of course."

"A written statement, giving the facts known to us, to be lodged with my lawyers and yours."

"Yes, anything of that nature." Ivo's face burned with excitement, the energy he had kept in leash now seemed to fill the room. "Dave, we'll have to move fast. Will you 'phone Miller and ask him to have the 'plane ready in half an hour, to take five passengers to Durban? The dog will have to come too." He turned to me. "Lennie, a great part of this will rest on you. Do you think you can do it?"

"Yes." Now the decision was taken, I'd stopped being afraid, and my mind felt fresh and strong. "There's something else. I think I know why Kate was killed, and maybe I know how."

The light eyes sharpened. "Do you? Then tell us on the way down." He glanced at his watch. "We'll be at Kolumbe by midnight. Time to sleep there, and make our arrangements tomorrow. I think if we say eight o'clock tomorrow night, at the shack? Dave will get in touch with each of them."

"What," said Evan, "if they refuse to come?"

"They'll come," said Ivo, and his smile had ferocity in it. "Dave will invite them to a farewell party for Kate Falconer. They'll come."

XXXIV

W E S P E N T T H E next day at Kolumbe farmhouse, complet-
ing our plans, and at nightfall went down to the shack.

I took a great deal of care about dressing for the party. I
wanted to look as much like Kate as possible. None of my dresses
was any good, but I found a pair of black velvet pants that
weren't too mod, and a white pleated blouse, and over that I put
my black suede jacket. I fixed my hair the way Kate fixed hers,
turned under on the shoulders. Just before we left I went down to
the barn and fetched Freya, put on her hood and secured her to
my wrist with a silk jess.

The others were waiting for me by the Volvo. Evan drove,
because I had Freya. Nobody spoke much on the way to the
estuary. I had a sort of idea that one or other of our guests might
take it into his head to arrive before time, but when we reached
the shack it was empty and quiet.

I checked that everything was ready, as I'd left it that morning;
the old table of scrubbed pine in the middle of the living-room,
with thirteen chairs round it. I put out thirteen wine-glasses, and
brought the wine from the cooler to the serving-table just behind
my own chair. I set out Kate's favours. Finally I opened the
folding doors between living-room and verandah, so that the
whole area was one.

The four of us sat on the verandah and watched the moon come
up blood-red from the sea. The closeness of the river made Freya
restless, so I took off her hood and secured her cord to the rail,
leaving her free to move right along it. At a quarter to eight, we
heard the first car turn off the main road and cross the bridge
over the river.

It was the Kandells' maroon Mercedes. Percy Kandell and
Mortimer and Hilary Silke climbed out and came up the steps to
where we sat. Mortimer led, waddling on his short legs, and his
wicked blank little eyes fixed first on Gretha and then on Ivo.

"Do the police know she's here?"

"No, they don't."

"Kidnapping's a capital offence, y'know."

"So is murder," I said.

Morty's mouth jerked, and he swung round, wagging a vicious hand at me. "Any nonsense from you, Missy, and I'll take you to law, understand? I'm here to protect my interests, that's all. Don't try and cook up anything against me or Hilary, because I won't have it."

Hilary wasn't listening to him. Her eyes were fixed on Freya. "What's that, a hawk?"

"A Peregrine falcon." As I spoke Freya batted with a clatter of wings, her great golden eyes shining. Percy Kandell, who was moving towards me in a smooth rush, thought better of it and stopped beside his daughter.

"A pretty bird," he said, and Ivo Hamilton laughed 'softly.

"Is that all you have to say, Percy? No pious text to offer us? No little deal to suggest?"

Percy's brows lifted. "I don't follow you, Mr Hamilton."

"I mean neither you nor Morty is going to buy your way out of this one. So don't waste your breath."

As he spoke, Silke had stepped past to scan the living-room, the river-banks, the estuary. Over his shoulder he addressed Ivo. "Who've you got here?"

Ivo smiled at him. "Shame on you, Morty. I came alone. This is a party, just a few of us getting together to remember an absent friend."

Silke waddled towards him. "I'll tell you plain, Hamilton, I didn't come here to remember anyone. I came because I'm a reasonable man, like you. I want to stop this thing dead. I don't want my wife bothered by reporters, I don't want all that again. Now without saying any more I suggest that we all put down whatever's necessary to fix it. Admitting no liability, of course. You and I have had our differences in the past, but now's not the time to bear grudges. Someone set us up with stuff in the press. That means there's a price. If that little cat over there knows what it is, let her say, and we can think it over, and if it's reasonable we'll put down the sum in exchange for a legal agreement that that's an end of it. What do you say?"

"I say that's a very neat attempt to make me admit complicity. No deal, Morty."

Silke shrugged. "Go to hell, then."

From the shadows near the rail, Hilary spoke, and her voice had twice the power and twice the venom of her husband's. "Nobody's going to blackmail us, I can tell you. If Miss Bryant starts anything, she'll be sorry. I knew Kate Falconer. I could tell things about her."

"You knew Kate," I said, "and she knew you. A cuckoo, she made you, short legs, big round tail, lazy and parasitic. She knew you, Hillary."

"Now wait a bit," Percy sounded hurt, "you can't talk to us like that. We came here in a friendly spirit, to talk things over, but we can change our tune, you know. There's the police. They'd like to hear what happened to Miss Corbitt, I've no doubt."

"Don't be a fool." His daughter cut him short. "And keep out of sight, there's a car coming."

This time it was the Sharveys' Jag that bumped off the track and entered the clearing. As the passengers alighted, Ivo switched on the outside light. The new arrivals checked in its sudden blaze, Sharvey squinting between spread fingers, Nell behind him with her arm round Nick. Then Sharvey turned to lift Nick's portable chair from the boot. Brother and sister came slowly on across the turf. At the foot of the steps, Nell raised her head and saw Gretha.

If what followed was acting, it was a masterly performance. For a moment Nell stood transfixed. Then with a cry she stumbled up the steps, arms stretched. Ivo barred her way and she thrust him aside in a frenzy of impatience.

"Gretha! Gretha darling, are you all right?"

Slowly, in a movement infinitely forbidding, Gretha raised her hands palm forward. "You told me she was sleeping," she said. "You told me lies."

Nell halted. Her mouth sagged in despair. Then, as she turned from Gretha's accusation, she caught sight of me, and at once her body stiffened in the old authority.

"How could you have allowed this?" she said. "You must have known she was alive. All this time, you've let us suffer, when a word, a 'phone call would have set us at ease."

I said nothing. After a moment she made a small, helpless movement. "I don't understand. What have we ever done to you, to deserve such cruelty?"

"What harm did Kate do you?"

Nick spoke behind Nell's shoulder. "Come. This has to stop. Gretha, my dear, we're taking you home. Come now, with Nick."

Gretha swayed. Nick's hand beckoned her. "We'll go home," he said. "We'll light a fire and sit and look at the albums. You remember how we used to do that?" He was offering a treat to a child, but the child shook her head and pulled her fists up to her breast as if some cold wind bit her to the bone.

"Cory Bergen came," she said. "Cory Bergen's dead, do you know that, Nick? Like Kate." She smiled. "They lit a fire for Cory."

Sharvey shouldered between them to stand before me. His hands caught my wrists.

"You have to stop it, he's right. She's mad."

"No one can stop it," I said, and as if on cue, the third car swung its headlights into the clearing. Johan Dessels climbed out and came up the steps.

I went to meet him. I didn't want him to talk. I held out my hand in formal greeting, and he took it, with a small precise bow. His pale eyes went round the assembly, noting each one of us, flickering a little at sight of Gretha, resting with cold intensity on Ivo Hamilton. "This one I don't know."

"Mr Ivo Hamilton, of Hamilton Developments."

Dessels gave a brief nod and looked back at me. "I did not wish to come, but I have a certain standing. What affects me affects others. I wish to protect myself if there is need. Is there?"

"That's what we have to discuss tonight," said Ivo, moving forward. "I think if you'll all come inside, we should begin our talk."

⑨ ⑨ ⑨

175

XXXV

F ROM THE HEAD of the table I indicated where each of them should sit; Nick Corbitt in his wheelchair on my right, with next to him Cory Bergen's empty place; Derek Sharvey, Nell Sharvey, Gretha; at the far end, facing me, Evan Cruikshank; Ivo Hamilton at bottom left, then Johan Dessels, Dave in Greco's chair, Mortimer Silke and Hilary. Percy Kandell sat directly on my left.

When they were seated, I took the wine decanters from the serving table, and sent them round. The eleven faces shone beneath the central lamp, restive, shrewd, wary. Beyond them lay shadows, the mutter of the river and the more distant surge of the sea.

In the silence my own voice rang too loud. "A toast, Ivo?"

He raised his glass. "How about the one Kate chose? 'Absent friends!' "

Nell Sharvey sent a horrified glance at the empty chair beside her brother. Mortimer Silke caught his wife's outstretched hand.

"Never mind the toasts, Miss Bryant. I want to know what we're here for?"

"A reunion, Mr Silke. A wake, a business discussion. Whatever you like to call it."

Silke began to bluster but Johan Dessels forestalled him, leaning forward to tap the table with a precise and fussy gesture. "Please. Wait. Certain things are obvious, we can save ourselves argument. The coincidence of these arrangements is too great." His thick hand indicated the placing of the chairs, moved to touch the favour that lay before him. "Kate made these. You know about them? Gretha has told you?"

"She told me she collected them from the table after Kate's last party."

"I see. How strange. Such a small detail. I had forgotten about them until you showed me that example, last Wednesday. Then, of course, it came back to me." His pale blue gaze shifted from me to Ivo. "This gentleman was not present, nor his nephew, nor Dr Cruickshank. The rest of us, yes."

"What are you trying to do?" Derek Sharvey's voice was unsteady. "Suck up to teacher?"

"Please don't be childish. We attended a party. That is no crime." There was bland warning in Dessels' tone. "Why attempt to conceal what appears to be common knowledge?"

Nick Corbitt stirred in his chair. "I agree. It's time to be frank. Miss Bryant has brought us here to discuss Kate's death. I think we must hear what she has to say."

"I have to say," I answered, "that each of you contributed to her death, and each of you conspired to conceal the facts of that death."

"Hard words." Nick sounded weary, almost bored. "Can you be more explicit?"

"I can. In 1946, my mother died and Kate came back from Europe to look after my father and me. She felt her loss very deeply. It was a bad time for her, a bad time for all of you. You, Mr Corbitt, were just back from the war. You were ill, broke and unemployable. A normal family would have got out of the cart by selling the house, but your family was not normal, not on that subject. You and Nell felt you had a God-given right to live in Michael Crescent, to receive from other people respect and homage and the luxuries you enjoyed. Nell married Derek Sharvey because his money kept the old illusions alive. Sharvey was a bright boy and he was going to make a packet. Only one thing looked like holding him back, and that was his partnership with my father.

"My father was no financial brain. As long as he had my grandfather to advise him, things went all right, but when the old man died, my father began to make mistakes. He ran up debts, and he cost his firm a lot of money. The whole future of the Sharvey-Corbitt set-up was endangered. The old friendship across the garden fence wore thin, and a new crowd gathered in my father's house. Some of them were Kate's friends, but more were sharpies aiming to live the sweet life. One of these was Percy Kandell. He'd done some work once for Sidney Falconer, he was in the building trade like my father, it wasn't difficult for him to

177

latch on. He had a daughter he hoped to push into society, and he also planned to make a lot of money out of the Falconers. He knew where the money was, but he couldn't work out how to get to it. That problem was solved for him by the arrival of Jean-Charles Greco.

"Jean-Charles was what nobody else in the Crescent could claim to be, a really high-grade crook. He was wanted by certain authorities in Europe, he needed a breathing space, and cash. He was looking for contact men. When he arrived in South Africa he got in touch with the Kandells . . . he'd met Hilary in Switzerland . . . and they introduced him to Mortimer Silke who had some capital and plenty of ambition. These four made a plan and set about carrying it out.

"One man, Evan Cruikshank, warned my father against them, but was told to mind his own business. After that, Greco and his crew had free run of the place.

"Greco's first move was to buy Derek Sharvey. I don't suppose it was difficult. Sharvey had no old-fashioned scruples against double-crossing a partner. He was cut in on the deal. His job was to persuade my father to accept Greco's proposition. It took a few weeks, but finally he succeeded.

"Once the deal was set up, Greco's next problem was to keep Kate from finding out about it. He was smart enough to know he couldn't leave her completely in the dark. He got my father to tell her he was going to sell the Falconer property in Michael Crescent, that Greco and Silke would form a company to develop the land, and that the Falconers and Corbitts would both have large holdings of shares. Kate accepted the story. She trusted my father, and at that time her mind was full of other troubles, my mother's death and her own love affair with Ivo Hamilton.

"So there we have it. A phoney deal to cover the real one. Everything going just the way Greco wanted it. Then something happened to put the whole scheme in danger. Kate decided to turn her annual Hallowe'en party into a launching of the new project. She invited her guests and made a pottery token for each of them."

I picked up the favour lying in front of Nick Corbitt and held it up.

178

"Amazing, isn't it, how much a trinket like this can tell? For instance, about what Kate thought of each of you. Shrike, skua, dove. She knew you pretty well. It's a pity she didn't judge you more harshly while she had time.

"Another strange thing; there was no token for herself. Yet there was one for Ivo Hamilton, a man none of you had met, certainly not the sort of man Greco would risk cutting in. My view is, Kate had already made up her mind to marry Ivo. His share and hers were represented in a single token, that of the eagle, which mates for life.

"But the most interesting question, for me, is the part the Corbitts played in all this. Kate made tokens for all of them, and for Bergen as well. In other words, they were part of the business deal that Greco was staging. Yet is it possible that Nell Sharvey and Nick Corbitt would agree so meekly to the sale of the Falconer house? They'd resisted for years, why should they knuckle down now? Did all or one of them guess the deal was phoney?

"Twelve people were invited to Kate's party. Of those, I believe two were completely loyal to her interests; Gretha Corbitt and Ivo Hamilton. The rest cheated her. Two I think regretted their actions and drew back. The rest went on, stripped her of everything, even life.

"There had to be a motive for that bigger than a few acres in Michael Crescent. There had to be big money involved. That was what Greco came looking for, and Percy Kandell told him where to find it.

"Percy, you see, worked with a brick and tile company. He knew ceramics. He also knew where to find the biggest clay deposits in the southern hemisphere, clay of several colours and the finest quality, clay that was close to the water and power and transport that a big industrial development demands. What Percy and Greco worked out between them was a way to get ownership of Kolumbe."

⑨ ⑨ ⑨

XXXVI

A RIPPLE WENT round the table, an edging closer, the ritual dancers closing in to the moment of sacrifice. My hands felt thick and cold and my mouth was dry with hate. I felt the way Kate must have done, the moment she learned what her friends planned to do. I fixed my eyes on Evan, because he alone had never failed her.

"Kolumbe is an obsession with my family," I said. "Not the farm, that's a living, nothing more. It's the sanctuary that matters. This shack, the estuary, the bush and the birds. To me Kolumbe is the most beautiful place in the world. My grandfather spent a fortune to keep it from profiteers and land-thieves. He formed the Kolumbe Wild Life Company to protect it. He couldn't know that that step would make it more vulnerable.

"Under the terms of my grandfather's will, the town house in Michael Crescent was left to my mother, Deirdre. Kolumbe sugar-farm was divided between Kate and Deirdre. Most of the capital in the bank went to Kate.

"But the crucial bequest was Kolumbe Sanctuary. When my grandfather formed the company, he kept two-thirds of the shares and made the rest available to the people of Kolumbe village. On his death, he divided his own shares between his daughters. They were young, he expected them to have children. It never occurred to him that circumstances could take the control of the sanctuary out of Falconer hands.

"But in 1945, my mother died. Her shares in the sanctuary passed to my father. So the position was, one third of the shares lay with my father, one third with Kate, and the remaining third, the vital third, had been distributed among the farmers and shopkeepers of Kolumbe district.

"That was the situation Greco found so interesting. He knew quite well that anyone who might have acquired a high percentage of the public-issue shares . . . say twenty per cent . . . could hold the balance of power between Ralph Bryant and Kate Falconer. If such a holder, and Ralph Bryant, could be persuaded to sell their holdings to Greco, then Greco would own over fifty per cent of the stock. He would be able to decide the fate of the whole Kolumbe estuary. In two years the sanctuary could become a flourishing brickfield with a huge industrial potential.

"Greco made some enquiries. He found that when my grandfather formed the company, the richest landowners in our district were the Dessels family. They farmed next to Kolumbe. What more natural than for them to buy in Kolumbe shares? Dr Dessels, it's true, isn't it, that by 1946, your holdings in Kolumbe were something like twenty-three per cent."

Johan Dessels shifted to face me. His right hand lifted to touch the sweat on his temple. "If you've checked..." he shrugged. "Yes. Twenty-three per cent."

"And Greco approached you, late in 1946, and invited you to sell him the shares?"

"Yes."

"You decided to accept his offer?"

Dessels said nothing, and I went on, "You decided to accept, not because you needed the money, but because you were suffering an emotional crisis. You were in love with Kate Falconer, and you knew you were losing her. Your jealousy had driven you almost crazy. You'd lost all sense of dignity and reason. You haunted Kate's home, made a fool of yourself before her friends, neglected your work. You'd known Kate since childhood, and you understood something very important about her. You understood that anyone who loved her had one permanent and unchanging rival. Kolumbe. She loved the place more than she loved most human beings, more than she loved you. You began to believe that if Kolumbe was taken from her, she might find more room in her life for you. Perhaps at the back of your mind was the idea you might blackmail her, somehow force her to come back to you by threatening to destroy Kolumbe?"

Dessels' control broke. His plump hands struck the table and he looked as I'd first seen him in my flat, murderous. "What right have you to talk of blackmail? The shares were mine, to sell as I chose. Was it right that she should value a few morgen of mud and bush higher than me? Kolumbe was all she thought of. Sometimes I wanted to kill her . . ." He checked, his mouth sagging in an oddly childish alarm, and then whispered. "I didn't. I didn't kill her." Tears misted his eyes and he blinked them away. "It was no good. At the end, I found I couldn't hurt her."

"You went to her?"

"Yes, about a week before the end. I planned to say . . . I don't know what, blackmail if you like, but when I was there with her, I told her the truth, everything. I told her Ralph was going to sell his shares, and that I'd promised mine. I warned her against Derek Sharvey. I hoped that when I'd spoken, things would be good between us, the way they were before, but she was angry, so angry. You don't know what it's like, to love someone and have her look at you like that. My heart froze, I was utterly deserted."

He seemed on the edge of tears, and Evan looked up with sharp contempt. "You were deserted? What about her? She'd lost you, Ralph, Sharvey. Can't you see that when you salved your own grubby little conscience, you left her with nothing? Which of us was she to trust after that?"

"She trusted us." Nell Sharvey met Evan's challenge with dignity, her strong hands folded on the table, her body erect. "Kate knew she could trust us."

"Could she, by God? You'd have sold a dozen Kolumbes, Nell, to keep your toe in Michael Crescent, and Nick would be right there with you. Elegant dinners and your invitation to King's House, that's what counted with you. You showed that fast enough when Ralph sold the house."

Her mouth was haggard but she wasn't beaten. "I knew nothing of Kolumbe being sold," she said. "Nor did Nick. And I repeat, Kate never doubted any of us. Ask Dr Dessels, if you don't wish to accept my word."

Dessels nodded. "Kate said nothing at any time against Mrs Sharvey, or Nick." He turned to me. "You can believe that."

"I do," I said, and laid aside the trinket I still held. Light struck through my wineglass on to the peacock's tail, spangling it with colour so that it seemed alive. "Kate felt she could trust the Corbitts absolutely. That's why she let the party go on as planned."

$$\mathcal{G} \quad \mathcal{G} \quad \mathcal{G}$$

XXXVII

"I F K A T E H A D been a more ordinary woman, she'd have called the party off, perhaps gone to a lawyer. But she wasn't ordinary. She had no conventional morals, only a personal morality. She loved intensely and hated just as intensely. She took risks that ordinary people don't take.

"When Johan Dessels told her what was happening, she spent several days thinking what she should do. By October 30th her mind was made up, and that night she spoke to my father.

"You'll remember that that was the last time she was seen in Durban. There was a party at the house, the place was full of friends, Corbitts, Sharveys, and others. Evan Cruickshank was there too, on one of his rare visits, and he spoke to Kate. He found her worried because, she said, she had 'something unpleasant to do'. Later, Evan heard her talking to my father in the drawing-room. He said, 'we have to think of the child,' and Kate answered, 'Yes, we must do just that'. She told my father to think of 'what Deirdre would have wanted for her'. She said, 'If you must sell, don't let it be her heritage.' To Kate, the Falconer heritage was certainly not a house in town. It was Kolumbe, and Ralph knew it. Before Kate left home that night, she'd come to terms with my father. He'd agreed to cancel the deal with Greco, and sell the Michael Crescent property to another buyer. Kate also told him the Hallowe'en party was cancelled. She wanted to deal with the people who'd used him, and she could do that better without him there.

"She took an overnight bag and drove out of town, to Kolumbe. She stayed at the farm. That is confirmed by Dr Dessels, who followed her out. Dr Dessels asked her for the last time to marry him, and she refused. Dr Dessels told me only a few days ago he never saw her again, a lie that is now exposed, since he saw her with the rest of you, on Hallowe'en."

I reached out my hand for my glass and found it empty. Percy Kandell started to rise from his chair, but Ivo was already up, moving to take the decanter from the serving table. Kandell sank back with an uneasy movement, and Ivo smiled at him.

"No one's leaving yet, Mr Kandell." He leaned over my chair and refilled my glass and moved on down the table.

"I wonder," I said, watching Percy's shifting glance, "how you all behaved towards Kate, that last time? Can you remember, Mr Kandell? Did you feel happy, looking forward to the money you were going to make out of her? Or did you find her different, did you suspect that something was not quite right? I'd like to know what you thought because by all accounts you're an observant man with an excellent memory."

Percy's tongue came out and touched his lower lip. He tried a smile that somehow slipped and became a grimace. "I don't remember. There was nothing unusual. We came here as friends, doing her a favour, that's all. We had her interests at heart, whatever you and the Doctor say."

He stopped abruptly as Morty Silke's hollow eyes fixed on him, then finished lamely, "There was nothing wrong."

"Not true, not true." The voice was Gretha's, and her white face leaned accusingly towards Kandell. "They were here, the Others, the Wicked Ones. They came from the river, smelling blood, they waited in the shadows and listened to the laughter."

"Whose laughter?" Ivo prompted her and she turned her feverish stare on him.

184

"Theirs." The swift arc of her hand described the whole table. "They laughed, they were proud, they were rich with secrets against her. I told her, 'Go away, the place is evil,' and she said, 'It will soon be over.' He warned her too. He felt it." A finger stabbed at Johan Dessels and his big body shivered.

"Yes, I did. She wouldn't listen."

"And the room," I said, "it was like this, the table, the favours, the wine at the side?"

He nodded. "Just the same." He seemed to have passed some limit of his powers, his face had a sick and swollen look. "The favours were set out. I looked at mine, I saw it was an ostrich, a bird without wings. I was hurt, such a small thing." His glance went to Ivo. "We can't all be eagles. Well, that's past. I have won my own place, my own honours."

"But you allowed Kate's place and honour to be destroyed." Ivo spoke harshly and Dessels flinched.

"Kate was dead. What could it matter what people said of her then?"

"What would have happened to your repute," I said, "if she'd lived? Did you feel safe, Doctor? Did you feel sure she'd keep your share in what was done, quiet? Or did you fear the story might get out? Cheating a friend is hardly the qualification for eminence, is it? You had a motive for murder that no one else at the party had. You knew that Kate knew. You'd felt the force of her anger. The others still believed themselves safe."

"I was safe," he cried. "She promised me. She promised, here in this room, that I was forgiven. Ask them. They heard her. It was only the guilty she wished to punish."

"And who were they?"

"Greco. Silke. The Kandells, and Sharvey. She named them."

"When?"

"At the end. I think it was at the end. I can't remember. I'm ill, I can't stand this."

"You can remember. Tell it as it happened."

"We sat." He wiped a hand over his forehead. "It seemed a long time. There was food and wine. Kate sat there, where you're sitting. She watched. All through the meal, while they talked and laughed, she watched, she led them on, she let them talk about the

185

new company as if she suspected nothing. She was like a hawk above a chicken coop, waiting her time. Her eyes looked strange. Then, at the end, she said, 'Fill up the glass, Nick, I want to propose one last toast.' She stood up in her place, and raised her glass. She said, 'To Kolumbe'. They all drank. She didn't sit down again, but set her glass aside and spoke to Greco. 'That's the last throw, Jean-Charles,' she said. 'The game's over. Kolumbe isn't for sale, tonight, or ever.'

"Greco just sat there waiting, as if he was puzzled. Kate said, 'Johan and Ralph have decided not to accept your offer. You're finished here.'

"Greco smiled at her. 'Finished is a big word,' he said. And she said, 'I mean it, Jean-Charles. You'll leave town tomorrow, you and Silke and Percy and Hilary. If you're not out of here by noon, I shall see the right people learn enough to wreck you. By the time I've done no one on this sub-continent will advance you a shilling.'

"He stared at her for a moment, and then he laughed. 'You're a fighter, sweetheart,' he said. 'Marry me and we'll make ourselves a fortune any way you like. You can keep Kolumbe.'

" 'I mean to,' she told him. 'Without your help. And now you can get out and take your friends with you.'

"Greco got up. He came round the table and he stood close to Kate and touched her cheek with one hand. 'One thing,' he said, 'one thing you should learn. Count the winners in the other guy's hand. I'll leave town because you can make it bad for me if I stay. But you'll keep your pretty mouth shut, because if you don't I can make it bad for your friends. Think of the buzz in Michael Crescent if people hear the Sharveys and the gallant Major Nick were all set to skin you.'

"Kate just shook her head at him. 'I can deal with Derek. Don't try and slander my friends, it won't do you any good. I advise you to go home and pack, you've only thirteen more hours.' Greco did what she told him. He said, 'Come on, Morty,' and Silke and the Kandells followed him out of the door."

A slight perplexity touched Dessels' face. "I found it very strange," he said.

"That they went so easily?"

"That Kate let them go so easily. One moment she seemed ready to annihilate them, the next...I don't know...her anger was gone. Sharvey too, she hardly said anything to him. When Greco and the others had left, she looked at Sharvey and said, 'Ralph gave me a message for you. He'll dissolve the partnership. His lawyers will take care of it. He won't do more, for Nell's sake. But I'm warning you, if you ever come near us again, you'll get more than you can handle.' Then she turned away from the table, and walked to the couch over there and sat down with her head on her arms. I thought she was crying. I went over to her and touched her hand. It was very cold. I said, 'They've gone, Kate. It's finished. Are you all right?' She said, 'Just tired. Where's Nell?' Nell came and sat beside her and put her arm around her. Kate murmured something and I stooped down to listen. She said, 'Don't worry, Johan, go home,' and then she turned her head aside as if the light hurt her. Her eyes looked..." again Dessels paused with that puzzled expression.

"'She looked'," quoted Ivo softly, "'like a cat in the dusk'. In other words, her pupils were widely dilated. Haven't you ever seen the effects of a massive dose of morphine, Dr Dessels? But perhaps Nick Corbitt will describe them for you. He knows the drug better than any of us, don't you, Nick?"

XXXVIII

"And so we come to it!" Nick leaned back in his wheelchair and surveyed us with a sort of smiling contempt. "The final idiocy. I've sat here and listened to your farrago of nonsense because that was the only way I could deal with it once and for all." His swollen finger stabbed at Ivo. "You have made a slanderous statement. Repeat it and I will have pleasure in taking you to court. As for Miss Bryant, I overlook her flights of fancy because she is young. The rest of you..." his pale lashes flickered in the direction of Mortimer Silke... "may be glad to hear the true facts, if only to arm yourselves against further attack.

"Kate Falconer did not die of narcotic poisoning. She did not die at this shack. She died in Kolumbe River as the inquest found, and it was an accidental death by drowning. After Jean-Charles Greco left with his friends, those of us who remained were naturally in some tumult of mind. My sister Gretha was so distressed by what had happened that she became seriously ill, and has never fully recovered. My sister Nell was faced with the accusations against her husband. You can imagine her feelings. Our one thought as a family was to get home as fast as possible.

"We could see that Kate was suffering severely from shock. Clearly we could not leave her alone at the shack. We tried to persuade her to come back to town, but she refused. Finally we took the only course left to us. We drove her up to the farm and left her there. She was perfectly well when we left her, though still very emotionally upset. I don't know at what stage she decided to take the boat out on the estuary, probably it was early the next morning. It was something she often did, you know, when she wished to calm her thoughts. I think she went out early on Sunday, when no one was about. The tide was high and the river in flood. She capsized the boat and was lost. You can blame me, if you like, for leaving her at Kolumbe. Nevertheless my actions were those of a friend."

188

"Such a friend," I said, "that you went back to town and pretended you hadn't seen her for two days. You let the scandal spread that she'd gone off with a lover. You allowed the court to censure my father for negligence, and when he put the house up for sale you fought him to the last ditch."

Nick hunched his shoulders. "Think what you like. Those are the facts of her death, as Nell and Derek can testify."

"I expect they'll have to." Ivo's voice was brisk. "You see, I intend to repeat my slanders. I shall say that Kate died in this shack. Sometime during that last evening, you realised she'd found Greco out. You knew Kate's temper. You knew she was going to blow the lid clean off. There was going to be an enormous scandal. You were going to lose not only the money your fingers itched for, but your cherished role of returned hero. That panicked you. You decided that you couldn't afford to let Kate live. You were next to her at dinner, you poured the wine, and you had a pocket full of soluble morphine, the quick action pain killers you always carried.

"You killed Kate, and it was only when she was dying that you began to realise your own danger. There was going to be an enquiry and a post mortem, unless you could find some way of getting rid of Kate's body.

"That was something you couldn't do alone, because you lacked the physical power, but you had three helpers, people who stood to lose as much as you if you were caught. You had Cory Bergen to carry Kate's body on to the marshland and bury it. You had your sister Nell to bully and threaten her husband into becoming an accessory after the fact, and you had Sharvey to take Kate's boat out to Kolumbe Island and swim back at low tide.

"That far you were lucky. But there was one other witness here that night, and that was Gretha. The shock of what she saw affected her mind. You were glad of that. It kept you safe. As long as her brain was clouded, you let her alone. But recently she showed signs of remembering. So you sent Bergen into her flat to finish her too. A pity that Bergen had to pay such a high price in your cause, wasn't it?"

Nick's chin sank on his chest. He looked old and shrunken and wicked, but there was no tremor in his voice. "I'm afraid you've allowed yourself to be fooled by the jabber of a madwoman. Do you imagine any sane person would believe Gretha's evidence?"

Gretha sprang to her feet. "It's true. I saw him carry her out. I saw him, and I'll tell."

Nick never even glanced at her. Instead he turned on me a look of glittering malice. "If she speaks, I shall have her certified. Is that what you want for her, to end her life in an asylum?" He raised a hand to Nell. "My dear, I really think it's time we left."

"Very well." She took hold of the chair's handgrips. "Derek? Are you coming?"

Sharvey shook his head in silence.

Nell drew the wheelchair back from the table, swung it through the door and out on to the stoep. I started forward, but had taken no more than a couple of steps when Ivo's arm closed round me. "No, Lennie. There's nothing we can do."

I can't tell you what it was like, standing and seeing the two of them walk away as free as air. I wanted to strike them down, and by the tremor in Ivo's muscles I knew he did too. But it was Gretha who moved.

She ran out on to the verandah, mouth wide, hair streaming, and hurled herself at Nell. Nell stumbled and wrenched round to grapple with her. The wheelchair spun wildly towards the verandah edge, crashed into the central pillar and flung Nick out against the rail. The old wood cracked but held. I saw Nick straighten, begin to take a step, and then swing his head aside in terror at the whirr of Freya's wings.

For an instant she hung above him, golden, shining, and then she struck. Her talons sank deep into the flesh of his face and he plunged backwards on to the rail, balanced there, legs flailing, and toppled into the river.

I've never known whose was the last cry I heard; the cry of the man as the flood tide caught him, or the cry of Freya as she spiralled, trailing her broken cords, into the hungry eye of the moon.

XXXIX

T HEY DIVED FOR him for a long time, Ivo and Dave and Derek Sharvey, but it was no use. It was five days before his body was washed up on the beach, far south of Kolumbe. There were a lot of stories about his death, but suicide was the most widely accepted. Everyone knew he'd been in pain for a long time.

He was accorded a funeral with military honours, and the papers published a picture of Nell, looking serene and noble in her mourning.

I don't know what she will do, alone in that big ruined house. Evan says she never leaves it, but the Peak Hill work is moving very fast. In a year or two there won't be much left of Michael Crescent.

Gretha is with Polly and me at Kolumbe.

Dave Leatherhead came out to see us at the farm yesterday. He leaves for Europe in a day or two, on a six weeks' trade mission. He asked me to marry him and I refused, and he said, "I suppose it's Ivo you want?"

I told him I don't know what the hell I want, not yet.

It's difficult to explain. I shared Kate's life for a while, and a little of her death. It's going to take me some time to climb back into my own skin.

So for a while I'll be quiet. Live here at Kolumbe, take Freya out hunting, work. I've started on a model of the Pel's fishing-owl. It's good, I think.

One day I'll be able to sit on the verandah at the shack and watch the sunset, and it will be just the sun going down and nothing more, and I'll be just Lennie Bryant and nothing more.

That will be the time to think about the future.